Finding Freedom

An Addy Classic
Volume 1

by Connie Porter

★ American Girl®

To my grandmothers,
Adelle Houston and Mary Jemison Dunn,
for the way back to my Addy

For Mr. Zimmerman

And for my niece Tia Porter

Beforever

Beforever is about making connections.
It's about exploring the past, finding your
place in the present, and thinking about the
possibilities your future can bring. And it's about
seeing the common thread that ties girls from
all times together. The inspiring characters you
will meet stand up for what they care about
most: Helping others. Protecting the earth.
Overcoming injustice. Through their courageous
stories, discover how staying true to your own
beliefs will help make your world better
today—and tomorrow.

TABLE *of* CONTENTS

Whispers of Freedom

ddy Walker woke up late on a summer's night to hear her parents whispering.

She thought no more of their quiet voices than of the soft chirping of the crickets in the woods just beyond the little cabin. Often she awoke to her parents' whispering. Addy liked the sound. It made her feel safe, knowing her mother and father were close by.

A small fire glowed in the hearth as the last coals burned down from the fire Momma had used to cook supper. Usually Addy liked the warm glow of the coals in the darkness. It was the only light in the windowless cabin. But tonight it just made her hotter. Sweat crawled down her small body like ants. The stiff, dry cornhusks stuffing her pallet poked through their thin covering, sticking her. Her older brother Sam lay on his own pallet near her feet. Addy could see his dark face in the firelight and hear his regular breathing. Her baby sister Esther lay next to her. Esther's steamy breath was blowing on Addy's face. Addy loved Esther, but it was too hot to be close to her tonight. Addy tried to wiggle away from the baby. When she turned from Esther, her parents stopped talking.

"Hush, Ben," Momma said to Poppa. "I think Addy woke up."

Addy kept her eyes closed, but she could hear the rustle of cornhusks when her father got up. His feet softly crossed the dirt floor. She opened her eyes just slightly as his shadow passed over her, covering her and Esther and Sam. Addy felt protected inside of it. She wanted to ask, "Poppa, what you and Momma talking about?" But she kept her mouth shut. When her parents started talking again, she listened.

"That child asleep, Ruth," Poppa said to Momma, returning to their pallet. "She tired out. They had the children out in the fields half the day worming the tobacco plants."

"Ben, listen to me," Momma said. Her voice was serious. "I don't think we should run now. The war

He got a hot head and a hot mouth. Sam done run off once, and now he want to go fight in the war. All he talk about is going north to fight for freedom. If Sam don't watch it, he gonna be getting us all in trouble."

Addy didn't like what she heard. She remembered when Sam had run off the year before, shortly before Esther was born. He was tracked down by Master Stevens's dogs and brought back. He was tied to a tree and beaten with a whip by Master Stevens. Addy screamed and cried, but her parents did not. They had blank, empty faces that made Addy angry. When the beating was over, Sam's back was covered with blood. Poppa carried him back to the cabin, and Momma and Poppa cleaned the blood from him. Finally Addy yelled at her parents, "Y'all don't care about Sam at all! Y'all not even crying." As soon as she said it, she felt bad.

"Come here," her father had said softly. Addy went to him, ashamed to look at his dark, stubbly face. She held her face down, but her father lifted it and wiped away her tears. "Just because you don't see us crying and carrying on don't mean we don't care. It don't mean we ain't crying, either. Me and your momma crying on the inside. We ain't always free to show our feelings on the outside. But on the inside we is free. There's always freedom inside your head, Addy."

Freedom. That was what her parents were talking about tonight. But they were talking about a different kind of freedom. They were talking about the kind of freedom a slave had to run away to get.

"If Sam take off by himself a second time, we might never see him again," Momma said in a worried whisper. "I want us all to be together."

Poppa didn't answer right away. Then he said, "Uncle Solomon told me in the field today that there's a set of railroad tracks about ten miles after the river near the Gifford place. We follow them north till they cross another set of tracks. Where they cross, there's a white house with red shutters. It's a safe house. An old white woman live there, named Miss Caroline. She gonna help us. We only got to get that far," Poppa said.

In the dark, Addy hugged Janie, the small rag doll Momma had made for her, the doll she slept with every night. Her parents' talk about running away scared her. She had never heard them talk about it before. Whenever Sam talked about escaping, they told him to hush up.

"If we get caught, Master Stevens gonna split us up for sure," Momma said, her voice shaky.

"I figure ain't nothing for sure," answered Poppa, "but we got to take our chances while we got 'em. You can't go backing out on me now."

"I'm not backing out," Momma said. She sounded cross. "I'm just scared. You want to go all the way to Philadelphia. I ain't never been no farther than the Gifford plantation. What if we get lost from each other?"

"We gonna go together and we gonna stay together. God will watch over us. You got to believe we gonna make it north." Poppa sounded sure and strong. Addy knew he could protect them, no matter what.

"Let's just wait a little longer. When the war over, we all gonna be free. All of us right here," Momma said again.

But Poppa was firm. "I hurt when I see Addy toting heavy water buckets to the fields, or when I see her working there, bent over like a old woman. Sam already fifteen, but she a little girl, nine years old, and smart as they come. She go out in the morning, her eyes all bright and shining with hope. By night she come stumbling in here so tired, she can hardly eat. Esther still a little baby, but Addy getting beat down every day. I can't stand back and watch it no more. We can't wait for our freedom. We gonna have to take it."

Momma was quiet again. Addy wasn't thinking about the heat of the cabin, her prickly pallet, or Esther's hot breath. She was waiting for her mother's answer. None came. She heard her father rise. He went to the hearth and covered the coals with ashes.

When Addy heard him lie down, her eyes popped open, but now Addy could see nothing. There was no light in the cabin. In the thick darkness, Addy knew she had heard a secret that she must keep to herself no matter how hot it burned inside her. She could feel Esther's breath on her back. Turning to face her sister, she moved close and put her arms around her. The baby's breath did not feel too warm now. Addy was glad Esther was there on the pallet with her.

As Addy fell asleep, the only voices she could hear in the night were those of the crickets in the woods.

Sold!

CHAPTER 2

Early the next morning, Addy was in the tobacco field worming the plants. She and the other children moved from row to row, carefully pulling green, wiggling worms from the leaves. The worms were as fat as her fingers, but Addy tried not to think about them. Instead, she dreamed about the kind of freedom Momma and Poppa had talked about the night before—the kind slaves ran away for. She saw herself learning to read and write. First, she'd write the names of everyone in her family. She saw herself wearing fancy dresses with lace, nothing like the rough cotton shift she always wore now. Poppa would get paid for his work and buy so much food they would never be hungry. He would buy cloth for her fancy dresses and Momma would make them for her.

By eleven o'clock the sun was high overhead, and
Addy felt as if she'd worked all day. She had just finished worming her rows when it was time for her next
chore, taking water to the field hands. The full bucket
of water she carried almost pulled her arm from her
shoulder. As Addy struggled with the bucket, sweat ran
down her dark face and soaked the neck of her shift.
But she liked this chore because she sometimes had a
chance to see Sam or Poppa. On this day, she saw Sam.
As usual, he had a riddle for her.

"Riddle me this," said Sam. "What's smaller than
a dog but can put a bear on the run?"

Addy thought hard as Sam took the dipper from the
bucket and poured some water over his head.

From a few rows away the overseer snarled, "That
water's for drinkin', boy."

Addy saw a scowl come over Sam's face. He mumbled, "Even a horse got to stop and cool off sometime."

"I better get on," Addy said, worried that the overseer might come over to them. He carried a whip.

"Naw," Sam said, his face softening. He was as tall
as Poppa, but he was skinny. When he smiled, Sam still
looked like a little boy. "I ain't done drinking yet, and

you ain't answered my riddle. What's smaller than a dog but can put a bear on the run?" he repeated.

He took a drink while Addy thought. She looked up to see where the overseer was. He had gone off in another direction. Addy crinkled up her eyebrows and said, "A skunk?"

"You right! I don't know about you. You too smart for me, girl. Pretty soon you gonna be riddling me," Sam said.

"Real soon," said Addy, smiling at her brother.

Addy wanted to tell Sam what she had heard their parents talking about the night before. But the escape plan was so daring and dangerous, she could not share it with anyone, not even her brother. If her parents had wanted her and Sam to know, they would have told them. So Addy kept the secret inside and moved down the row to give the next field hand a drink. When the bucket was empty, she headed toward the kitchen to help Auntie Lula serve dinner to Master Stevens.

The kitchen was a small brick building behind the big house. Addy hurried there, afraid she might be late.

Auntie Lula was ready for Addy to work as soon as she stepped into the building. "Wash your hands good," she said, "and take that tray of food and water to the dining room."

"Yes, ma'am," Addy answered. She liked Auntie Lula. She was an old woman, old enough to be Addy's grandmother. Her skin was light and her rusty red hair was streaked with gray. She had a soft, open face, but sharp green eyes that could see right through you. Auntie Lula looked after Addy and her family. She gave them medicine when they were sick. One Christmas she had made rock candy for Addy and Sam.

The dinner Auntie Lula had cooked for Master Stevens smelled so good, Addy ached for a bite of it. All she had had for breakfast was cornmeal mush, and that was all she would have for dinner. Maybe Auntie Lula would hide away a few scraps for Addy to eat today.

Addy washed and dried her hands, and then picked up the tray and hurried to the dining room. Master Stevens was sitting at the table talking with another white man—someone Addy had never seen before. She set the food on the table and then poured water for both men. As they began to eat, she took her place standing quietly in the corner.

"You got that little girl trained real good," the man said to Master Stevens. "She looks like a smart one."

"I got them all trained real good," said Master Stevens. "That's why it's such a shame to let any of them go."

Addy's stomach turned when she heard Master Stevens say those words. *Let any of them go?* she thought. *What he mean, let go?*

"But I have twenty-two slaves to clothe and feed this winter," Master Stevens went on, "and you know how hard it is with the war. I need the money."

Addy stared at the floor, but she was listening very closely. She let her face go blank and empty.

"This boy you got for me," said the man, "how can I be sure he won't run on me, too? I know he's run before."

"I taught him a lesson with the whip last time he ran off," Master Stevens answered, "and you'll have his father, too. His father can control him."

They were talking about selling Sam and Poppa!

Addy just knew they were. Her father had been right. Master Stevens was going to split up their family!

"Hey, girl, more water," the strange man said, turning to Addy.

Addy hurried to pour him more water.

"You sure you don't want to part with this one?" the man asked Master Stevens, patting Addy on the head.

Addy's hand shook. She wanted to pull away from his touch, to scream. But the blank look was frozen on her face. She filled the man's glass and started to pour water for Master Stevens.

"I'm not looking to sell her," Master Stevens replied, "but I know the price for good house servants is going up every day. Maybe when she's a little older, I'll let her go, too. By then she might fetch a price as good as her brother. She's just too young now."

Addy was listening so hard, she forgot to pay attention to her task and filled Master Stevens's glass too full. Water spilled on the table.

"See, I told you this one's too young," Master Stevens said to the man. To Addy, he said sharply, "Girl, go get a rag and clean up this mess!"

"Yes, sir," Addy said. She was glad to have a reason to run back to the kitchen. She burst through the door. "Auntie Lula," she panted. "That man fixing to take Sam and Poppa with him! Master Stevens gonna sell them!"

Auntie Lula looked worried, but when she spoke, her voice was calm.

"If that be true, we don't have much time," Auntie Lula said. "Listen to me good, now. Take your bucket and run to the well. Fill the bucket and head right to the fields where your brother and father at."

"But I already took water," Addy said.

"Hush up, child," Auntie Lula hissed. "You a smart girl. Act like you think it's time for the afternoon water. Walk right out to Sam and your poppa and tell them what you heard. If that man really coming for them, it's the one chance they got to run. I'll go back to the dining room. Now you get!"

Grabbing her bucket, Addy ran to the well. She ran as fast as she could, her bare feet kicking up little puffs of dust, her thick braids beating against her shoulders. *Please don't let him take Sam and Poppa. Please, God,* she prayed silently as she ran.

When Addy came to the well, she filled her bucket. She tried to run with it, but the water splashed crazily over the sides. With less than half of it left, she headed toward the fields, walking as fast as she could. Her throat was dry. *Sam! Poppa! Where you at?* she screamed inside. Outside, her eyes desperately searched the huge field.

Addy was looking for Sam and Poppa and didn't see the overseer until he stepped right into her path. "Hey, girl!" he barked at her. "What you think you doing?"

Addy was so startled, she dropped her bucket. "I come to bring the afternoon water," she said.

"It ain't time for their afternoon water, you stupid girl. Get on out of here."

"I thought it was," Addy stammered.

"Don't give me back talk," the overseer snarled.

Addy felt frantic, but she said nothing more. She picked up her bucket and ran back to the kitchen. When she got there, she saw her mother and baby Esther with Auntie Lula. Addy rushed to Momma and threw her arms around her.

"Momma, they selling Sam and Poppa. I tried to

warn them, Momma. I tried," she cried, burying her face in her mother's shoulder.

"I know you did," her mother said softly. "Auntie Lula told me."

"Master Stevens and that man headed for the barn," Auntie Lula interrupted. "Maybe they got Sam and your poppa there."

Addy's head jerked up. Maybe there was one last chance. Maybe she could still warn Sam and Poppa. Addy raced out the door and headed for the barn.

"Addy!" Momma called after her. "Wait!"

But Addy did not stop. She was not thinking, not praying, just running, running, running. When she came to the field, she saw a wagon. Sam was in it, bound and gagged, shackled hand and foot. Master Stevens, the man from the dining room, and two other white men as big as Poppa were standing next to the wagon.

"Sam!" Addy cried out when she reached the wagon. "Oh, please, Master Stevens," Addy begged. "Don't let them take Sam."

"Get out of here, Addy," Master Stevens ordered. He had a whip in his hand.

Addy stopped where she was. Then she heard a deeper voice.

"Addy, go on now." It was her father's voice. But where was he? She looked down and then saw him lying on the ground, being chained by the overseer. Poppa's face was covered with dirt, but it was calm. She ran to him, falling on the ground next to him. "Oh, Poppa. No. No!" She threw her arms around him. He looked up at Addy.

"Everything's gonna be all right, honey. You go on," he said. There were no tears on his face, but Addy knew he was crying inside.

"Get back, girl," Master Stevens barked. Addy heard his whip crack. She felt a lash of fire on her back as if she had been burned. But still she held on to Poppa.

Master Stevens growled at her. "I told you to get. Now get before I whip you again." He reached for Addy and yanked her away from Poppa.

Addy fell backward into her mother's arms. Momma held Addy close, both of them crying. This time, even Momma couldn't keep the pain hidden inside.

A New Plan

I t was late on Friday afternoon, nearly a week after Sam and Poppa had been sold. Addy and the other children were worming tobacco plants. They were to work their way down the long rows, turning over every leaf to find the worms and kill them. It was a job Addy hated. She didn't even like looking at the worms. To kill them, she had to either squish them with her hands or squash them under her bare feet.

Addy's mind was not on her work. All her thoughts were about Poppa and Sam. *Hey, I got a riddle for you, Sam,* she thought to herself. *What's heavy as a full pail of water, but still empty, empty, empty? Give up? It's my heart.* She peeled the worms off some plants but forgot to look under the leaves of others. When she came to the end of her second row, the overseer came along behind her to check her work.

Addy was just starting the next row when she saw the overseer storming toward her. He had his whip in one hand. She turned to run, but he got to her before she could take a step. Addy raised up her hands, thinking he was going to hit her.

But he did not hit her. He dropped the whip and pulled Addy's hands down from her face, yanking her toward him. Holding her wrists in one of his large hands, he opened his other hand. Addy saw what he held—live worms. Worms that Addy had missed. The overseer forced open her mouth and stuffed the still-twisting and wiggling worms inside.

Addy began choking.

"Eat them!" the overseer growled. "Chew them up—every last one of them. If you don't, I'll get some more."

Addy gagged as the worms' juicy bodies burst in her mouth.

"That'll teach you to mind your work," the overseer snapped. He shoved her away. Addy crumpled to the ground as he turned to leave.

It was dark when Momma came home to the cabin that night. She had baby Esther on her hip. There was no fire in the hearth. Addy lay curled up on her pallet. Her face, arms, and legs were streaked with dirt. Her feet were covered with mud.

"Addy, you awake? Get up, honey," her mother said, lighting a candle and then placing Esther down on the pallet. But Addy did not even look up.

"Addy," her mother said in a voice as soft and warm as the glow of the candle. "What happened to you?" She sat down on the edge of Addy's pallet and touched her head gently.

Addy opened her eyes. They were red. As she told her mother about what the overseer had done to her, she started to cry. Momma lifted Addy's head onto her lap. "I hate them, Momma. I hate white people," Addy sobbed.

"I don't want you to hate nobody," Momma said, stroking Addy's hair. After a while, she got up to get some water. When she came back, she began washing the tears and dirt from Addy's face.

"Don't you hate them, Momma?" Addy asked.

"No, I don't hate white people," Momma answered. "Honey, if you fill your heart with hate, there ain't gonna be no room for love. Your brother and Poppa need us to fill our hearts with love for them, not hate for white people."

"But Momma, that overseer and Master Stevens, they hate us," Addy said bitterly. "Why white people hate us and treat us wrong?"

"Addy, all white people don't hate colored people. Not all of them do us bad. Master Stevens was wrong to sell Sam and Poppa and to whip you. But Addy, people can do wrong for such a long time, they don't even know it's wrong no more. What's worse is when people hurt each other and don't even care they hurting them. Like that overseer. He a mean man. That's what hate do to people. I don't want you to ever be that kind of person."

Esther began crying. Addy reached over and handed her rag doll to the baby. Esther quieted down.

"Addy, there something I need to talk to you about," Momma said slowly, "something serious. You listening to me? Your poppa and me talked about something before Master Stevens sold him and Sam.

Poppa was worried about the war, and times getting hard . . ."

Addy knew what her mother was going to say. With all that had happened in the past week, Addy had almost forgotten about the secret she had been keeping, but now she let it out. "You and Poppa planned for us all to run away," she said.

"How did you know that?" Momma asked.

"I heard y'all talking one night," Addy answered. "I didn't mean to listen, but I couldn't help it."

"Then you already know we planned to go north," said Momma. "Well, we still going."

"What about Poppa and Sam?" Addy asked. "Shouldn't we wait for them to come back for us?"

"They ain't coming back here ever again, no matter what," Momma replied. "Poppa's plan was to go to Philadelphia. He told Sam about it the day after you heard us talking. I aim to stick to that plan, and we leaving tomorrow night."

Addy looked into her mother's thin face. There were fine lines of worry around her brown eyes.

"Tomorrow! But what if we get caught?" Addy asked, her voice shaking.

"There ain't no choice, honey. I never thought
Master Stevens would break up our family after your
poppa and me served him our whole life. But I was
wrong." Momma shook her head. "After what he done,
Addy, I can't keep you safe here no more. I'm scared
that man who bought Sam and your poppa might come
back for you. I can't stop him if he do. I ain't gonna sit
here and wait for him or anybody to come take you
from me."

Esther started to cry again, and Addy patted her
gently. Then she said, "Momma, I'm scared, but I want
to go to freedom. Esther want to go, too." She turned
to her baby sister. "Don't you want to go to freedom,
Esther?" Addy asked. "Don't you want to go find Poppa
and Sam in Philadelphia?"

"Addy, go to my pallet and get what's under it,"
Momma said.

Under Momma's pallet were two large kerchiefs
and some clothes. They were not clothes for a woman
and a girl, but for a man and a boy.

"Momma, what we gonna do with these?" asked
Addy.

"I'm gonna pack them kerchiefs with some food,

a drinking gourd, things like that. We wearing the clothes," answered Momma.

"We gonna be disguised?" asked Addy in surprise.

"They a disguise, but they more than that," Momma explained. "Auntie Lula and Uncle Solomon got them for us. When Master Stevens send out his dogs after us, it's gonna be hard for them to track our smell if we got on somebody else's clothes."

"Auntie Lula and Uncle Solomon should come with us, Momma," said Addy. "Poppa say Uncle Solomon know where the safe house is. They should come to freedom, too."

"They too old to come to freedom, Addy. They can't run," Momma said. "They would slow us down."

"Esther can't run neither, and she coming," Addy said.

Momma lowered her head. Addy knew something was wrong. Her mother would not look at her. Then Addy saw tears on her mother's face.

"Momma, what's the matter?" Addy asked.

"I may as well tell you now, honey," her mother said, her voice slow and sad. "Esther ain't coming with us."

Addy could not believe her ears. She must not have heard right. She picked up Esther and held her close.

"No, Momma," Addy said. "We ain't leaving Esther."

"Addy, did you hear me?" Momma's voice was soft but firm. "Your sister is staying here."

"But why? Poppa said we was all going," Addy insisted.

"Honey, it was different when your poppa and Sam was going with us. They could help carry Esther. Now I got to carry her by myself."

"I could help, Momma. Let me help. I could carry her," Addy begged.

"Besides," Momma went on, "Esther might cry any time. Her crying would give us away."

"I could keep her quiet, Momma, I just know I could," Addy said. "I'd let her hold Janie while we was running."

"Addy, Esther can't come," her mother said.

Addy hugged Esther again.

"This the hardest thing I ever had to do in my life," Momma went on. "I love Esther as much as I love you and Sam, but we can't take her. Auntie Lula and Uncle Solomon is gonna keep her. She just a baby, so Master

Stevens ain't gonna sell her. He can't make no money selling a baby."

Addy cradled Esther in her arms, gently rocking her back and forth. The three of them sat quietly for a long time. Then Momma broke the silence. "The war ain't gonna last forever. When it's over, we gonna get Esther back. Our family will be together again. Lay down now," Momma said, blowing out the candle.

"Momma, can we all sleep together tonight?" Addy asked.

"I'd like that," Momma said.

Addy, Momma, and Esther crowded onto Addy's pallet. Esther was sandwiched between Addy and Momma. The baby held tight to Janie.

Addy moved as close to Esther as she could to feel the baby's warm breath on her face. She put her arms around her tiny sister. Addy tried not to cry, but itchy, hot tears were running down her face, and she didn't bother brushing them away. She felt her mother's arms around both her and the baby. Beyond, from the deeper darkness of the woods, Addy heard a single owl hooting in the night.

Into the Night

he next night, after it was fully dark, with not a streak of orange or red in the sky, Auntie Lula and Uncle Solomon came to Addy's cabin. Addy and her mother were in their disguises, with their kerchiefs packed. The well-worn clothes were baggy on them. Esther was sleeping on Addy's pallet.

Uncle Solomon had two hats with him. One was a straw hat that he gave Addy's mother. The other, a felt hat, he placed on Addy's head.

"Now, there's magic in your hat," Uncle Solomon said to Addy, trying to cheer her up. Addy did not feel like smiling.

"Don't you believe that hat got magic?" Uncle Solomon asked. He snapped his fingers near her left ear. "Why, look what's come out your ear. You must've forgot to wash behind it. Look at this half dime I found there." He handed the coin to Addy.

Addy reached behind her ear. "How'd you do that?" she asked.

"Shhh," Uncle Solomon said. "It's magic. You hold on to that half dime. You gonna need it where you going. Freedom cost, you hear me? Freedom's got its cost."

"Come on, Solomon, they ain't got all night," Auntie Lula said. "Look here, I got some food and things for you," she said, handing Addy's mother a small sack.

Addy's mother put the sack into her kerchief, and then she bent down to pick up Esther. Esther woke and began to fuss.

Addy watched Momma as she hugged the baby hard and kissed her over and over. She searched Momma's face for tears, but there weren't any, not on the outside at least. Addy kissed Esther, too, and stroked her head. "Don't worry, Esther. We coming back for you," she whispered softly as she handed her rag doll to the baby. "You hold on to Janie until I see you again," Addy said. Then her mother gave Esther to Auntie Lula.

"We gonna take good care of Esther. Don't worry," Auntie Lula said, looking into the baby's eyes as she held her. "She gonna be right here when you come back for her."

Uncle Solomon gave Addy and Momma some final advice. "Go fast as you can at night and hide during the day. Every time you see water, go through it. A creek, a river—I don't care if it ain't nothing but a puddle, go through it. That way you won't hardly leave no scent for the dogs to pick up on. And watch out for them Confederate soldiers. They dressed up in gray uniforms. They can be mean as snakes, and if they catch you, they gonna bring you back to slavery."

"God be with you," Auntie Lula said as Addy and her mother turned to leave the little cabin. Esther began to cry as they slipped out into the damp, warm night and ran into the woods. Addy looked back to catch a final glimpse of her baby sister, but tears blurred her sight.

The full moon shone in the eastern sky, looking like a half dime shining in the bottom of a well. At first, the moonlight shone through the tall pines, filling the forest with a silver light. Addy and her mother ran from shadow to shadow like a deer with her fawn. But as they moved deeper into the woods, only a small glimmer of moonlight made its way through the thick branches of the trees. There were dark, eerie shadows everywhere, and it was hard to see. Momma took Addy's hand as they hurried along, stumbling over vines and stumps hidden by the darkness.

Addy expected to hear the comforting night sound of the crickets that she always heard at the cabin, but the deeper they got in the woods, the stranger the sounds became. Owls screeched high in the pines. The wind moaned like a wounded animal. Branches from saplings reached out for her, stinging her face as they slapped against her. A bat swooped down from the trees, its wings beating the air just above their heads. Suddenly a dark form stirred in the bushes ahead, moving toward them. Addy screamed and froze. Momma jerked to a stop and clamped her hand over Addy's mouth.

"Hush up," her mother whispered sharply. "You can't holler out."

The bushes moved again. Addy's heart beat very fast. Bump-bump-bump-bump. Bump-bump-bump-bump.

Slowly, Momma took her hand away from Addy's mouth. "It's only a possum or a skunk," she said calmly.

Addy let out a sigh of relief. "Momma, I ain't mean to holler," she whispered. "We left Esther behind because her crying might give us away. But I hollered louder than Esther ever could." Addy remembered what her father had said about not always showing your feelings. She would have to learn to keep them inside sometimes.

All through the night, Addy and Momma stumbled through the darkness. They waded through swampy places where their feet were sucked deep into oozing mud. They clawed through prickly vines. The thorns snatched at their clothes and dug into Addy's hands until they bled. Bare roots tore through the tough skin on the soles of Addy's feet. Once she stubbed her toe on a rock and fell down. But this time Addy did not cry out. All night long, she and Momma pushed on and on.

Just when Addy thought she could not go another step, the sky began to lighten. She could see Momma's

face for the first time in hours. It was streaked with
dirt. She touched her own face and felt dried blood on
her cheek from a cut below her eye.

"We better stop soon, Momma," Addy said softly.
"It's getting light out and somebody might see us."

"You right," Momma said. "We need to look for a
hiding place."

They went a little farther and found a small cave.
They crawled inside and huddled together, waiting for
sleep to come.

When they woke up hours later, it was hot. Mosqui-
toes buzzed around their heads, drawn to the stickiness
of their sweaty skin. Addy slapped at them, but it was
no use.

"You must be hungry," Momma said, reaching into
her bundle. She handed Addy a piece of Auntie Lula's
cornbread. It was hard and dry, but it tasted good to
Addy. She washed it down with a drink of water from
the gourd.

When they finished eating, Momma reached into
the bundle again. "I got something for you," she said.
Addy watched eagerly as Momma opened her hand.
In her palm was a small, shiny shell.

"I want you to have this," Momma said. "It's something me and your poppa been saving for you. This cowrie shell belonged to Poppa's grandma. She was stole from Africa when she was no bigger than you. None of her family was on the ship with her when she came here from across the water. She wore this shell on a necklace. Your poppa was gonna give it to you when you was older, but I think you should have it now, Addy. Your great-grandma's name was Aduke. That name got a meaning where she come from. It means 'much loved.' I saved her name for you, Addy."

Addy was silent for a moment. Then she looked into her mother's gentle brown eyes. "Momma, can I hold the shell tonight?"

"Sure you can. I got something special to put it on," her mother said, pulling a leather string out of her bundle.

"Momma, that's one of Sam's shoelaces," Addy said.

"I wanted you to have something of his, too," her mother said. She pulled the cord through a small hole in one end of the shell, knotted it, and then put it around Addy's neck. "Remember what I told you about the love you need to carry in your heart. It ain't nothing you can touch like this shell, but when you find your-self feeling sad or scared, you dip into that love, Addy. It's a well with no bottom, and it can give you strength and courage."

Addy rubbed the shell between her fingers. Its rounded top was smooth as soap. The flat underside was also smooth, except for the middle where the shell closed in on itself. There it felt like the teeth of a fine comb.

"My great-grandma must have been brave to come across the water all alone. I'm gonna be brave just like she was," Addy said.

"She *was* brave, Addy," Momma answered, "and you brave, too. But there's one thing different about you and your great-grandma. Her journey ended in slavery. Yours, girl, is taking you to freedom."

They sat in silence a long time, looking at the cowrie shell and thinking about someone they had never met.

Then Addy spoke. "Momma, do you think Esther gonna remember us?"

"That ain't easy to say. Babies don't remember much, but I got a feeling Auntie Lula won't let her forget," Momma said.

As Addy and Momma settled down in the cave to wait for sunset, Addy pictured Esther back on the plantation. She would be asleep now, curled up with Janie. Maybe she would be thinking about Addy.

When night finally came, Addy and Momma started out again. The moon lit their way until they reached the end of the woods, where they saw a flat darkness ahead of them. Then, before they could see water, they heard the rushing sound of it. They had come to a wide river.

"This got to be the river near the Gifford plantation that Poppa talked about," Addy whispered.

"We got to cross it," Momma said, her voice sounding scared. "We better stuff our hats and things in our pockets."

They stood on the bank of the river for a few moments, afraid to enter the foaming, angry water. Sam had taught Addy how to swim, but this water looked dangerous—and Momma didn't know how to swim at all.

Holding tight to each other, they started into the

water together. Addy picked her way along the squishy bottom, her feet slipping on the slimy rocks that were stuck in the mud. Once she tripped on a rock, losing her balance and pulling Momma with her. Addy felt her mother's grip tighten around her hand and realized again how frightened Momma was.

Pulling themselves up, they slowly made their way to the center of the river. There the current started to pull at them. It lifted them off the bottom and dragged them sideways. Hard as they tried to walk against it, the water was stronger than they were, and they were pushed farther and farther away from shore. Addy could hear Momma sputter as water filled her mouth and nose.

"Momma, keep your head up," Addy yelled as loud as she dared. "Just don't go under."

Suddenly a huge swell of water rushed against them, pulling Momma's hand from Addy's, dragging her away. Addy turned just in time to see her mother disappear beneath the churning water.

Addy wanted to scream, but she kept it inside. Instead, she drew in air, filling her lungs, and dove under the water. She struggled against the current, trying to stay close to the place where Momma had disappeared. She couldn't see a thing in the dark water. She felt around for Momma, but she found nothing. Addy's lungs began to burn. She was running out of air. Popping up above the water, she looked around frantically.

"Momma," she called, gulping for air. "Momma, where you at?"

Afraid no answer would come, she dove down again. This time she let the current push her while she dragged her arms through the water, searching for her mother. Suddenly, Addy was stopped by a fallen tree under the water. She groped among the branches, but their sharp ends jabbed and poked her. She kicked furiously to get away when suddenly her foot hit something soft. It was Momma, trapped in the branches. Addy braced herself against a large limb, grabbed Momma, and then pushed off against the tree with all her strength to bring both of them to the surface.

Gasping for air, the two struggled to the far shore. Clutching each other, they finally reached the shallows where the water calmed. Exhausted and breathless, they fell on the riverbank. When Addy could finally talk, she whispered, "Momma, is you all right?"

"You saved me, Addy," Momma said weakly. "You a brave girl."

Addy was shivering as she and her mother got up and slowly made their way into the woods. Their wet clothes stuck to them. Momma had lost her kerchief, and her hat was ripped. Addy pulled her own hat from her pocket. Other than being wet, it looked fine. She pulled it down tight on her head and thought, *Maybe it is a lucky hat.*

She reached to see if the cowrie shell was still around her neck. It was there, and something else was, too. It felt like a wet leaf. When she peeled it off, Addy realized it was a leech. She shuddered and quietly flicked it away.

Addy and her mother traveled for hours before Momma spotted the railroad tracks. Addy had never seen tracks before. They were shining silver, and they pointed the way north to freedom.

"These got to be the tracks your father talked

about," Momma whispered. "We got to be extra careful out here. There ain't hardly a place to hide."

They had seen no one since they started their escape, but tracks meant a train could come at any time. Travelers might spot them. They could trust no one.

Addy and her mother followed the path of the tracks in the moonlight. When the noises of the night were gone and birdsong began to fill the air, they found a thick clump of pine trees near a curve in the tracks. Gathering dead branches and brush, they made a shelter and crawled inside.

Addy could barely keep her eyes open. She was too tired to slap at the ants that crawled on her legs or swat at the flies buzzing over her head. She curled up and rested her head on her mother's chest.

"I'm real proud of you," Momma whispered as she gently stroked Addy's hair away from her face. Addy smiled. She could feel her mother's heart beating. It was a soothing sound.

Freedom Taken

 low rumble woke Addy and her mother. Addy thought it sounded like thunder. Then a light appeared far in the distance. Addy could see it moving toward her, getting bigger and bigger. It looked as if the moon had fallen from the sky and was rolling through the tops of the trees. Safe in the darkness, Addy and her mother crept out of their shelter just in time to see something Addy had only heard about. A train!

She could make out its shape charging through the darkness. The engine was spitting red sparks, and a ribbon of smoke ran along the length of the train. As it passed along a curve in the tracks, Addy watched its rear light disappear into the distance. But instead of moving away in a straight line, the train turned to the right. Addy was puzzled. Then she understood—the train had turned onto a set of tracks she could not even see yet.

"Momma, we here!" Addy said, a little too loudly. She lowered her voice. "The safe house has to be near the place where the train turned! We did it. We made it, Momma!" Addy threw her arms around Momma.

"I think you right," Momma said. "Let's go."

Addy and her mother ran hand in hand toward the place where the train had turned.

"We safe now," Addy exclaimed. "We going to Philadelphia."

"We ain't there yet," Momma said sharply. "Hush, now."

"We gonna see Sam and Poppa," Addy went on. "Then we come back for Esther, and the whole family be together again." Addy pictured them all in Philadelphia, living in a beautiful house.

"Freedom ain't that easy, girl," warned Momma. "Don't get your hopes too high."

But Addy didn't hear her. Spurred on by her thoughts of Philadelphia, she moved faster and faster, pulling away from Momma. Running fast, she felt the cowrie shell beat against her chest. She was going to freedom.

It was a long way to the place where the train had turned, but Addy was still running when she saw a small light. It looked like the glow of a lantern. Addy thought it must be in the window of the safe house. She raced toward it, her mother far behind. It was not until she was closer that she saw she was wrong. She stopped suddenly. The light was from a small camp-fire in a clearing near the tracks. A group of men were gathered around it. Addy could see them lying on the ground, sleeping. She was about to turn and run back the other way when she heard a gruff voice call out, "Who's there?"

Addy turned. She could see the face of a white man in the light of the fire. He had on a gray jacket and gray hat. He was a Confederate soldier, and he was staring right at her!

"Oh, it's you, boy. Bring me some water," the sol-dier said.

Although Addy knew he was looking right at her, she didn't think he was talking to her. He was talking to some boy. But what boy? Just then Addy remembered the disguise. *She* was the boy!

Desperately, Addy looked around. Then she saw a bucket of water. To get to it she had to walk right through the soldiers' camp. She saw another soldier on the ground stir. He rolled over. What if they all woke up and captured her?

Addy lowered her head, touched the cowrie shell briefly, and began to move. Inside she was shaking, but on the outside she was walking straight and strong past the sleeping soldiers. She picked up the bucket and brought it to the soldier.

"Train scare you, did it, boy?" the soldier asked.

Addy kept her head down and nodded.

"You'll get used to it after a while. Get on back to sleep," the soldier said.

Addy wanted to rush back into the woods, but she knew she couldn't. She acted as though she belonged in the camp. She walked to the edge of the clearing and lay down. The soldier lay down, too, and Addy waited a few minutes until she could hear him snoring. Then, as quietly as she could, Addy crept away from the soldiers and into the woods. *I got to warn Momma,* Addy thought. Just when she had gotten far enough away from the camp to start running, someone reached out and grabbed her.

It was Momma. She pulled Addy so close to her that Addy could feel the shell pressed between them. Momma held Addy for a long moment and then led her away.

When they were far from the camp, Momma spoke at last. "I was watching you with them soldiers, Addy, and I was holding my breath the whole time. But you did it, girl. You kept your feelings inside this time. Your poppa would be proud of you."

They walked farther along the tracks until they came to the place where two sets of tracks met and formed a silvery cross. A house stood just beyond the cross up on a little hill. It was white with red shutters. Poppa had been right.

To Addy it seemed that the house was just waiting for them. They did not have to run to it. They only had to walk and knock on the door where freedom was. It would open to them.

Addy and her mother crouched in the shadows, staring at the white house. There was no light from inside.

"Why we waiting?" Addy whispered.

"I don't know if it's safe," her mother said. "There might be more of them soldiers around."

"It's got to be safe," Addy said. "It's a safe house."

"Addy, it ain't that simple," Momma said. "Your poppa said a white woman live there. Them soldiers might be coming in and out of there. I don't trust them."

"But Momma, we got to trust the white woman. If we don't, where we gonna go?" Addy asked.

Without answering, Momma took a deep breath and stood, pulling Addy up with her. They slipped out of the shadows and walked to the house.

Momma tapped lightly on the door. No answer came. She tapped again, and still there was no answer.

Addy looked at her mother's face. It was calm and still. At last, a light glowed in the house. Through a small window, Addy could see the light of a candle move through the dark house. She heard the door being unlatched on the other side.

It opened, and an old woman not much taller than Addy stood before them. Her face shone in the light of her candle.

"Miss Caroline? Can you help us?" Addy asked.

Addy saw the woman's face twist into an angry scowl. "I thought I told you not to come here, boy. Go back and tell those soldiers I won't help them," Miss Caroline said. She started to shut the door.

Addy stuck her foot in the door to keep it from closing. "We ain't with them soldiers, ma'am," Addy said quickly, "and I ain't no boy." Addy pulled her hat off, revealing her braids. "Me and my momma running away to freedom. Can you help us?"

Addy saw the look on the woman's face soften. All the anger washed from it.

"Come in," Miss Caroline said. "Please come in."

Addy and her mother stepped inside. The woman quickly closed the door behind them and led them to the kitchen.

"My, oh my," Miss Caroline said. "Those are some fine disguises. I thought you were with those Confederate soldiers. They got here yesterday and sent a boy right over here to ask me for food. But I didn't give them one crumb. I don't cotton to those Rebels. You must be tired and hungry. I don't have much, and nothing fancy. But you're welcome to it. Sit down and I'll start a fire."

Addy and her mother sat watching the woman work. She seemed to be everywhere, starting the fire, dragging a tin tub next to it, heating a large pot of water, putting plates on the small table.

"Let us help," Momma said.

"No, you sit and rest. I know you must be tired," Miss Caroline said. "Who sent you here?"

"Uncle Solomon," Addy's mother said. "We trying to get to Philadelphia."

"Oh, Solomon," the woman sighed. "I've known him for over fifty years—since we were both children on farms that were next to each other." She served Addy and her mother some rice and boiled greens. Addy felt safe in this small, warm home. While Addy and Momma ate, Miss Caroline left the kitchen. When she returned, she had a bundle of clothes in her arms.

"These are clothes I save for runaways. After your bath, you find something that fits. You can rest here tonight. Then I'll take you to the coast. You can get a ship to Philadelphia from there. We have to leave before sunup—before those soldiers wake in the morning and come back here."

"Thank you so much, ma'am," Addy's mother said.

"I wish I could do something for you."

Addy went to her bundle and untied it. She took out the half dime Uncle Solomon had given her and held it out to the woman.

"Oh, I don't want money," Miss Caroline said, "and I don't want you to do anything for me. There's no need to thank me. You both are so brave to have escaped and come so far. It's thanks enough to know I'm helping you have a new life."

Addy and her mother took long, hot baths. The dirt from their journey melted off them in the warm water. That night, for the first time in their lives, Addy and Momma slept on a real mattress, not one full of itchy cornhusks. Addy tried to stay awake so she could think about how good it felt to be clean and safe, but she was too tired. She fell asleep in Momma's arms.

Before the sun came up, Addy, Momma, and Miss Caroline got ready to leave the small white house with the red shutters. Momma was dressed in a brown dress, Addy in a blue one.

Addy loved her dress with the dainty black bows on the sleeves. It was prettier than any she had imagined when she dreamed about freedom. Miss Caroline had found a pair of drawers and a straw bonnet that just fit Addy. After Addy tied the ribbon of the hat under her chin, she stood straight and tall for her mother to see.

"How I look, Momma?" Addy asked.

Momma's eyes filled with tears. "I wish your poppa could see you now, child."

Outside, Miss Caroline hid Addy and her mother in the back of her wagon and covered them with some old sacks. The wagon rocked gently as it pulled away from the safe house. Addy lay close to her mother. She reached to her neck and felt for the shell. Holding it tightly, Addy thought of Esther, Sam, Poppa, and even her great-grandma who had come across the water alone. They were with her, all of them. With the deep well of love in her heart, she could feel them with her.

"Momma, we done it," Addy said softly. "Just like Poppa said. We took our freedom."

A New Home

everal days later, Addy and her mother stood on a busy pier in Philadelphia. It was a hot afternoon at the end of August. Addy's boots pinched her toes and trickles of sweat ran down her back. She took Momma's hand and looked around nervously. *We finally here,* she thought. *Momma and me in Philadelphia. We gonna start our new life here. This where Poppa say freedom is.*

The pier was a noisy place. Huge crates hung from ropes overhead. They swung by clumsily as they were unloaded from ships. Addy cringed, thinking one of the ropes might break and a crate would come crashing down on her and Momma. A fishing boat had dumped its catch on the pier. Some of the fish were still alive. Addy saw their mouths moving as if they were sucking for air. Addy felt the way the fish looked, as though she couldn't breathe in the dirty yellow-gray air that smelled like burning fires.

Addy had never seen so many people in her life. It seemed as if everyone in Philadelphia must be on the pier. Some people bent under the weight of heavy trunks. Others had nothing. Some people stood quietly, looking lost. Others shouted out to people who were meeting them.

"I wish Sam and Poppa was here," Addy said as she saw a small girl being swept up in a man's strong arms.

"Addy, we by ourselves," Momma replied.

"I know, but wouldn't it be something if we was to turn around and they was here, just like magic?" Addy said.

"It would be something," Momma sighed. "I wish I knew where they was."

Addy heard sadness in Momma's voice. Addy knew Poppa and Sam were probably slaves on another plantation—unless they had been able to escape. But baby Esther was still at Master Stevens's plantation. Addy wished they had all been together when she and Momma finally made it across North Carolina to a hot, crowded boat that took them to Philadelphia.

The boat had just arrived minutes before. Addy felt lost in a sea of strangers. "Momma, you think we should be waiting someplace else?" Addy asked.

"The boat captain said to wait here, Addy," Momma said. "Somebody gonna come for us."

"Maybe we should ask somebody what them signs say," Addy suggested as she looked at signs around the pier.

"We ain't gonna do that," Momma said quickly, with fear in her voice. "We in the big city now, and we can't be trusting strangers."

I wish I could read, Addy thought. *Then I could help.* But she did not know one letter. As she shifted back and forth on her aching feet, Addy began to worry.

Maybe no one will come. What if we got to find our way around the city by ourselves? Where we gonna go?

Addy's heart started to race, but she tried to keep her face looking calm. She didn't want to worry Momma.

Nearly half an hour passed. The crowd had thinned out when Addy saw a woman and girl coming toward them.

Addy kept her eyes on the girl. She was about Addy's size. She skipped ahead of the woman and waved to Addy as if she were a long-lost friend. As she came closer, Addy saw a sunny smile on her face.

"I'm sorry we late," said the woman, who was tall and heavy-set. She reached out to hug Momma and then Addy. "I was told you was coming on the *Libby*, which is way down on pier thirty-five. Come to find out, you was on the *Liberty* here on pier three. I'm Mabel Moore and this is my girl, Sarah."

Sarah reached out and shook Addy's hand. "It's good meeting you," she said. Up close, her smile was even brighter.

Mrs. Moore went on, "We from the Freedom Society of Trinity A.M.E. Church, and we gonna take you to the church to see about getting you settled."

"We grateful," Momma said. "I'm Ruth Walker and this is my girl, Addy."

"Well, come on with us," Mrs. Moore said.

As they fell in step behind their mothers, Addy looked shyly at Sarah. Sarah's brown skin was the same color as Addy's. Her hair was as short as a boy's, and her faded dress reminded Addy of the shift she had worn back on the plantation. Sarah's big, dark eyes were so bright, Addy could see herself in them when

Sarah turned to her and asked, "Where'd you and your momma come from?"

"North Carolina," Addy answered. "We was slaves on a plantation."

"My family from Virginia. We was slaves, too," Sarah said. "My teacher, Miss Dunn, from North Carolina. Her family was slaves, too."

"They got colored people up here teaching school?" Addy asked. She could hardly believe it. Back on the plantation, she didn't know any colored people who could even read.

"They sure do," Sarah said. "Miss Dunn went to college and everything. You got to be smart to do that." Sarah looked at Addy. "You is coming to school, ain't you?"

"Momma say I can go," Addy answered.

"That's good," said Sarah. "We learn to read and write. We have spelling matches, learn our sums, and everything. We even study the war. You gonna like school. You'll see."

Just then they came to a busy corner. Sarah took Addy's hand. "I don't want you getting lost on your first day," she said.

Addy was glad to hold Sarah's hand. She hardly knew where to look as they walked down the crowded, narrow streets. She stared at the carts piled high with fruits and vegetables, heaps of coal, and bundles of rags. She looked up at the horse-drawn wagons and carriages that sped past them. She looked down so that she wouldn't step in garbage and horse droppings. She stared at all the people, black and white, old and young. Many of them wore fine clothes.

Sarah pointed to a street sign. "See that sign there?" she asked Addy. "It tell you where you at. We on Second Street now. When I come up here, I got lost loads of times because I couldn't read."

"Wish I could read," Addy mumbled.

"Not reading is nothing to be 'shamed about," Sarah said, giving Addy's hand a reassuring squeeze. "Miss Dunn will teach you to read. She taught me. And I can help you learn, too."

Addy smiled at Sarah. "I'd like that," she said.

"I'm gonna help you, I promise," Sarah said, smiling her sunny smile.

When they arrived outside the church, Addy was amazed at how big it was. And when they went inside, she could hardly believe her eyes. Addy had never seen such a huge place before. She stood in the middle of the center aisle and slowly turned around.

"That's a pipe organ," Sarah said, pointing to the back of the church. "It make real pretty music. The choir sit up there with it. And look, there in the front of the church. That's the pulpit for the pastor."

"What's that wrote over it?" Addy asked.

"It say, 'Peace be within thy walls,'" Sarah read.

Mrs. Moore led Addy, Momma, and Sarah down to the basement of the church and into a large meeting hall filled with people. The candles in the wall sconces gave the room a warm glow. Long tables were covered with platters of fried chicken, greens, biscuits, pies, and cakes. Addy had seen food like this only once before, a long time ago, when Master Stevens had a grand party. Sarah whispered to Addy that most of the people in the room were church members she knew. But some were slaves who had just arrived from the South. They were new like Addy and Momma. By the time Addy and Momma sat down to eat, it seemed they had been hugged by everyone in the room. Addy felt that they were being welcomed into a big family.

While they were eating, Mrs. Moore asked Momma, "What kind of work can you do?"

"I can sew some," Momma said. "Back on the plantation, I did mostly mending, but sometimes I made shirts and things like that."

Mrs. Moore's face brightened. "I know where you might find some work," she said. "There's a woman over on South Street named Mrs. Ford. She a white woman, and she got a small dress shop. She can be fussy, but she pay good, and I think she got a room you and Addy can stay in."

After the meal, Mrs. Moore left Sarah at the church while she took Addy and Momma to the dress shop just a few blocks away. The tiny shop was crammed with cloth, thread, ribbon, yarn, feathers, and boxes. A woman sat near the back, bent over her sewing. She looked up when they arrived.

"Good day, Mrs. Ford," Mrs. Moore said. The three visitors barely fit inside the shop. Mrs. Moore introduced Addy and Momma and said, "I think Ruth Walker would be a fine seamstress for you."

"I'll be the judge of that," Mrs. Ford snapped, looking over the top of her spectacles. "You know, Mrs. Moore, the last girl you brought here got married and left me soon after she started. I'm an abolition- ist and I want to help you colored people. But I have a business to run, and I can't take too many chances."

"Momma a real good sewer," Addy added bravely, "and we ain't gonna take off."

Momma squeezed Addy's arm, and Addy fell silent.

Mrs. Ford's sharp eyes looked at Addy and then at Momma. She said, "I'll hire you, Mrs. Walker—on a trial basis. A dollar a week to start. I run a first-rate shop here. Most of my customers are from Society Hill, and they expect the best. You'll have to do fine work, and I'll expect you to make some deliveries. If you can't do the work, I won't keep you on. This is a business, not a charity ward."

"Yes, ma'am," Momma said. Her voice was soft but steady.

"All right then," said Mrs. Ford. "I'll take you up to the room where you and your daughter can stay."

Addy, Momma, and Mrs. Moore followed Mrs. Ford up three flights of steep, dark stairs. At the top was a garret. Addy's heart sank. The room was dirty, stuffy, and hot. It was smaller than the cabin Addy's family had lived in back on the plantation. A table with two chairs stood in the middle of the room, and a bed had been pushed into one corner. There was a small stove. Then Addy saw something that made her feel better— a window that looked out over the street. Addy's cabin on the plantation had no windows.

"It's not much," Mrs. Ford said. "It's hot in the summer and cold in the winter."

"It'll be fine," Momma said quickly. She put her arm around Addy's shoulders. "We gonna make it a home."

Freedom?

ddy stood at the window of the garret, gazing out at the street below. A week had passed since she and Momma had arrived in Philadelphia, and nothing magical had happened at all. Back on the plantation, Addy had dreamed about being free in the North. She'd wear fancy dresses, she'd learn to read and write, she'd spend more time with Momma. She had imagined that everything would magically be better when she was free. But so far, freedom wasn't the way she dreamed it would be.

Momma worked long hours in the shop. She spent her day making dresses for rich women, working just as hard as she had on the plantation. But back there, if Addy didn't have a chore to do, she could find Momma and sit with her while she worked. Not here. Addy had gone down to the shop on Momma's first day. But

Mrs. Ford made it clear that Addy was not to be in the shop while Momma was working.

So Addy spent her days in the hot room in the attic. The window didn't bring Addy much joy. Sometimes a small breeze pushed through it, but the air was foul. Addy could smell soot, rotting garbage from the street, and the fishy scent of the harbor. The window let in all kinds of noises, too. Trains clanked in the distance. Ships in the harbor sounded their deep, lonely horns.

Although Addy didn't like being alone in the room, she was too scared to go out by herself. She didn't know her way around. She couldn't read the street signs, and the crowds of people in the streets frightened her. Sarah had told Addy that she once had seen a boy pushed into the path of a speeding wagon. Both his legs had been crushed.

The only time Addy went downstairs during the day was to go to the privy. Ten families used the same privy. It sat in the middle of a dark, filthy alley. The privy smelled awful, and the alley did, too. People threw all sorts of things into the alley—dirty water, table scraps. At night, rats prowled through the piles of garbage.

Addy had seen Sarah only once, at church on Sunday. Sarah's mother was a washerwoman and Sarah helped her, so she had little time to play. Addy longed for baby Esther, Sam, and Poppa more than ever, but she didn't tell Momma.

Addy was lost in her thoughts when she heard someone running up the stairs. She opened the door and saw Sarah.

"I'm so glad you here!" Addy exclaimed. "Ain't you got to help your momma today?"

"I do," Sarah said. "She sent me to the store for some bluing and a cake of soap. She said I could stop by here for a minute. And guess what?" Sarah went on. "Your momma said you could come with me."

Addy was so happy, she took Sarah's hand and they ran down the stairs. When they got outside, Sarah said eagerly, "School start next week. I can't wait."

"Me neither," Addy said excitedly.

"You can sit with me," said Sarah. "We got double desks, and you can be my desk partner."

"Good!" agreed Addy, though she couldn't imagine what a double desk looked like.

"My momma is letting me wear my Christmas

dress from last year to the first day of school," Sarah went on.

Addy looked down at her dress. It was the same blue one she had worn when Sarah met her at the pier.

"Do the girls dress real fancy at school?" she asked.

"Some do," Sarah answered. "There's this one girl named Harriet. She got lots of pretty dresses."

"It sound like she rich," Addy said.

"Compared to us she is," shrugged Sarah. "Her momma don't work."

They came to a curb and waited for a wagon to go by. It was the biggest one Addy had ever seen. The wagon was drawn by two horses and packed with people, some sitting, some standing.

"What kind of wagon is that?" Addy asked.

"It's a streetcar," Sarah explained. "Streetcars go all over the city to take people to different places."

"Let's get on it," Addy said as they crossed the street. "It look like fun."

"We can't ride it," Sarah said, "even if we had money for the fare, which we don't."

"You mean children got to ride with their momma or poppa?" asked Addy.

"No," Sarah said. "I mean they don't let colored people ride on that streetcar."

Addy looked confused.

"It's true," Sarah said. "There is a few streetcars for colored people to ride on. But we can only ride on the outside platform, even if it's raining or snowing. And they charge us colored folks the same fare they charge whites."

"That ain't right," Addy said.

"It ain't, but it's the way things is," Sarah said.

When Momma came to bed that night, Addy told her about the streetcars. "This where freedom supposed to be at," Addy said. "There ain't supposed to be things colored folks can't do."

"Honey, you right," Momma said, turning over the pillow so the cool side touched Addy's cheek. "But there's more to freedom than riding a streetcar. There ain't nobody here that own us, and beat us, and work us like animals. I got me a paying job. You can go to school and learn to read and write. When you got an education, you got a freedom nobody can take from you.

You'll still have it even if you never ride a streetcar."

"I wish you ain't have to work so hard," Addy said. "We got to buy everything now—food, candles, coal, matches. And it all cost so much."

"Freedom got a cost," Momma went on. "Just like Uncle Solomon told us before we left the plantation. It cost money and hard work and heartache." She kissed Addy's forehead. "Be patient, honey. Things gonna get better, I promise. Now, you go on to sleep. I got sewing to do."

The first day of school, Momma and Addy were both up before the sun. Momma had washed, starched, and ironed Addy's blue dress so that it looked like new. Now she braided Addy's hair in two braids and tied each with a ribbon that Mrs. Ford had given her from the end of a roll.

When Momma finished, she hugged Addy. "Do good in school now, Addy," she said. "You a smart girl."

"I'm gonna work hard, Momma," Addy replied as she hugged Momma back. Suddenly they heard some-one running up the stairs.

Sarah burst into the room without knocking. "You ready, Addy?" she asked. Sarah had on a dark green dress trimmed in white. It was old, but clean and carefully mended.

"You look real nice, Sarah," Momma said. She handed Addy her lunch pail. Momma had tied a scrap of green and white cloth to the pail so Addy could tell hers from other children's. Momma walked downstairs with the girls. "Y'all be careful now. Watch out for them wagons and streetcars, and don't talk to no strangers. Go straight to school and come right straight back here after."

"Don't worry, Mrs. Walker," Sarah said. She hooked arms with Addy. "I'm gonna look after Addy. I ain't gonna let nothing bad happen to her."

The Sixth Street School was a brick building near Trinity Church. Boys and girls had gathered on the steps out front. All of them were black, and they were all different ages. They were talking and laughing and playing. Addy felt scared, but she tried not to show it. She held tight to Sarah's hand as they walked past the other students and went into the building. Sarah showed Addy the way to their room, which was a classroom for boys and girls in the lower grades.

Addy felt more nervous than ever when she saw the classroom. It was crammed with desks. In one corner was a large black stove. On two walls of the room were huge black squares filled with writing. On another wall there was a large piece of paper filled with color-ful shapes. *What's that for?* Addy wondered. A group of children was already in the room, talking happily to one another and looking through books. Addy was worried. She knew those children would soon find out she couldn't read or write. Addy held on to Sarah's hand, but she wanted to break away and run.

Sarah's voice interrupted Addy's thoughts. "Here come Miss Dunn," Sarah said.

Addy watched as the teacher entered the room. Miss Dunn held her head high and her back straight. Her long skirts swung gracefully as she made her way across the room. She seemed to be gliding on air.

Miss Dunn smiled at Addy and Sarah. "Welcome back, Sarah," she said. "And who is your friend?"

"This here is Addy," Sarah answered. "She from North Carolina just like you, and she ain't never been to school before."

Miss Dunn put her hand on Addy's shoulder. "I'm so pleased you're here, Addy," she said. "You know, I never went to school until my family came north. When I started, some things seemed a little strange. You might feel a bit confused this first week, but you'll soon learn your way. I know Sarah will help you."

Addy smiled as Miss Dunn floated away. The teacher had made her feel much better. Suddenly, a bell rang and more children hurried into the classroom. Addy and Sarah sat down together at a double desk at the back of the room.

When everyone was seated, Miss Dunn said, "Good morning, boys and girls. I am Miss Dunn." She pointed to her name on the blackboard. "I know many of you, but I see some new faces. I want you children who have been here before to help the new students feel a part of our class. If we help each other, I know we will enjoy our year together. Tomorrow I will assign permanent desk partners."

Miss Dunn asked every student to stand up and state his or her name. Then she announced that the class would spend the morning copying from the board.

"Sarah," she said, "please help Addy copy the alphabet."

"Yes, ma'am," said Sarah.

Sarah was a patient teacher. She showed Addy how to hold her slate pencil and how to form the letters of the alphabet. Addy tried to hold her pencil the way Sarah did, between her thumb and first two fingers, but it kept slipping. Her letters looked shaky. Addy finally wrapped her entire hand around the pencil. Even then, the letters she slowly formed were squiggly and rough.

Miss Dunn stopped to look at Addy's slate. "You're doing fine," she said. Then she wrote something on one side of the slate. "This is your name," she said. "I want you to practice it."

Addy stared at the letters. It was the first time in her life that she had seen her name written down. Addy tried to copy the letters carefully. But her slate pencil broke because she pressed down so hard. The letters wobbled across her side of the slate in a crooked row. Addy erased them and started again. This time they looked more like Miss Dunn's letters.

Sarah looked at Addy's slate. "That's good, Addy," she said kindly. "I can read that plain as day. A-D-D-Y."

Addy had to smile. It had been a struggle, but she had written her own name, just as she dreamed she would. And she had found something she had not even dreamed of when she worked in the tobacco fields. In Sarah, she had found a friend.

Tested

he next morning, Addy's heart beat quickly when Miss Dunn announced the new seat assignments. "Addy Walker, you'll share a desk with Harriet Davis," she said.

Addy and Sarah looked at each other, and then Sarah blurted out, "Miss Dunn, can Addy stay with me? I been helping her."

"No, Sarah, I want Addy to sit near the front of the room. Clara Johnson will be your new desk partner. You can help her," Miss Dunn replied.

Addy rose slowly. She glanced back at Sarah as Clara slid into the seat next to her. Addy went to her new seat. She sat down next to Harriet and smiled shyly. Harriet did not smile back.

Harriet had light brown skin, and she wore her hair loose. She was wearing the most beautiful dress Addy had ever seen. It was light yellow and trimmed with rows of lace. Addy realized that this must be the girl Sarah had told her about.

"Do you know the alphabet?" Harriet asked. She had a thin, high voice.

"I'm just learning it," Addy answered. "Sarah was teaching me."

A quick frown crossed Harriet's face. "Sarah?" she said. "Sarah can hardly read herself! I'll help you. I taught myself to read when I was four. Miss Dunn put you with me because I'm the smartest one in the class."

"Sarah smart, too," Addy responded.

Harriet ignored her comment. "I'm named after Harriet Tubman. She helped run the Underground Railroad. You probably didn't know that. I know plenty of things like that. Now that Miss Dunn put you with me, I can teach you some things."

At lunch Sarah asked, "How you like sitting with Harriet?"

"She real smart and she got fine clothes just like you said. I wish I had a dress as pretty as the one she has on," Addy said.

"You know how much one of them fancy dresses cost?" Sarah asked.

"How much?" Addy asked.

"More than my momma and poppa make in a whole month," Sarah answered. "Your momma can't afford to make you a dress like that, Addy."

Addy's eyes opened wide. She had no idea one dress could cost so much. "Maybe my momma can find a way," she said. "Harriet's momma could afford it."

"I'm sick of talking about Harriet," Sarah snapped.

Addy was surprised by Sarah's reaction. "What's the matter?" she asked. "Don't you like her?"

"That ain't it," Sarah said, letting out a sigh. "Addy, Harriet don't like me. She all stuck-up. She think she better than other people. If your family ain't got no money, she don't like you. And you know my family poor."

"But Harriet was nice to me," Addy protested, "and she know my family is poor."

"Listen, Addy. She was only nice 'cause Miss Dunn told her to be," Sarah said firmly. "Harriet don't have no poor girls like us for her friends. She gonna try to make you her slave. She tried it with me when I came to school last year, but I wouldn't let her. That's why she don't like me. She gonna hurt you just like she hurt me last year."

"Well, maybe Harriet changed from when you first come up here," Addy said. "Harriet ain't gonna hurt me. She say she got plenty to teach me, and I got plenty to learn."

As the weeks passed, Addy's fascination with Harriet grew. Every day Harriet wore a beautiful dress. Each one seemed brand-new. And schoolwork came so easily to Harriet! She was always the first one in the class to finish her lesson, so she had time to look at Addy's slate and point out Addy's mistakes. Sometimes Addy didn't understand the corrections Harriet made. But questions seemed to annoy Harriet, so Addy saved her questions to ask Sarah at lunchtime or when they walked home together after school.

Addy worked very hard, and so she was discouraged after her first spelling test. Out of the twenty words on the test, Addy spelled twelve wrong. When Miss Dunn handed back Addy's test at the end of the day, she was encouraging. "Look how many words you got right, Addy. If you keep learning this fast, you'll be one of the best spellers in the class. Maybe your mother could help you with the words you missed."

"Yes, ma'am," Addy said softly. She didn't want to tell Miss Dunn that Momma couldn't read or write. And she didn't want Harriet to overhear her say it.

When Addy and Sarah were walking home after school, Addy said, "I ain't never gonna catch up. Younger girls can read and spell better than me. Maybe it's too late for me to learn."

"It ain't never too late," said Sarah. "You can't learn everything at once. Learning go slow. I didn't do so good on the test, neither. I should've studied harder."

"I studied hard and I still didn't do good," Addy said. "How many did you get right?"

"How many did you get right?" Sarah asked.

"I asked first," Addy said.

Sarah said, "Well, I got 'em all wrong 'cause I didn't study at all. My poppa can't hardly find work, so my momma and me been taking in extra washing. Sometimes I ain't got time to do my lessons."

"Maybe we can do our lessons together sometime," Addy said.

"I'd like that," Sarah said, sounding more cheerful.

Sarah left Addy at the door of Mrs. Ford's shop, and

Addy stepped inside. As she headed toward the stairs, she saw Momma sitting in the back of the shop. She was crying. "Momma, what's the matter?" Addy asked.

Momma dried her eyes on the sleeve of her dress. "You can come in, Addy," she said. "Mrs. Ford ain't here. She went out and left these packages for me to deliver. She wrote down the addresses on this here paper. I ain't dare tell her I can't read. She gonna be coming back soon expecting to see these packages gone, but I don't know where to take them."

"I can take them," Addy said. She looked at the addresses, but her heart sank when she realized she could read only one of them. Then an idea came to her. "Momma, Sarah can help. She can read way better than me, and she know her way around Philadelphia."

Momma looked doubtful.

"Momma, let me go catch up with Sarah. It's the only way," Addy begged.

"All right," Momma said after a moment. "But y'all be extra careful."

Addy grabbed the packages and paper and started running. She caught up with Sarah a few blocks away and explained the problem. Sarah studied the paper for a moment. Then she said, "I know where these streets is. Let's go."

Sarah hurried through the busy streets with Addy rushing along beside her. Sarah pointed to the street signs and read the names aloud for Addy. She showed her how the numbers on the houses went in order. After they had delivered the last package, the girls walked back to the shop.

As they walked in the door, Momma threw her arms around them. "Sarah, you been a big help. I don't know what we'd do without you," she said.

Just then Mrs. Ford returned. When she saw Addy and Sarah, she said, "What's going on here, Mrs. Walker? This is a place of business, you know."

"Yes, ma'am. The girls were just leaving," Momma said quickly. She squeezed Sarah's hand to thank her again. Sarah headed for home, and Addy hurried up the stairs to the garret.

That evening, as Momma was cooking supper, she sounded worried. "I ain't got a right to this job because I ain't been honest with Mrs. Ford. I gotta learn to read or find something else to do."

"I can teach you how to read!" Addy exclaimed.

Momma shook her head. "I think it's too late for me," she said.

"Sarah say it ain't never too late," said Addy. She took her spelling paper out of her satchel. "I got most of them wrong," she said, showing the paper to Momma. "But Miss Dunn say if you help me, I could be one of the best spellers at school."

"But I don't know how to help you, Addy," Momma replied. "I don't know the letters."

"I can teach them to you," Addy answered, "and I'll get practice from helping you."

Momma's eyes looked for a moment at the cowrie shell hanging around Addy's neck—the shell that had come from Addy's great-grandmother, who had been captured in Africa and brought to America as a slave. "All right, Addy. I'll try," Momma said. "Our family done faced tougher things than this. Ain't no change coming overnight, but by and by maybe we'll both learn."

Addy smiled at Momma. "Let's have our first lesson tonight."

As weeks passed and it started to get cool, Momma kept a small fire in the stove in the evenings. Sometimes when they made bread or meat pies for supper, Addy showed Momma how to spell words by forming letters with scraps of leftover dough. Momma loved to write *Sam, Poppa,* and *Esther.* "Seeing their names make me feel closer to them," she said. After they ate, they went over Addy's lessons. Addy taught Momma how to count, showing Momma what she had learned on the abacus at school by using beans on the table.

Every day Addy and Sarah went back and forth to school together, sometimes stopping to pick up colorful leaves or smooth chestnuts that fell from the trees. Sarah taught Addy how to read the names on street signs and shops as they walked along. One brisk morning as they passed by a grocery store, Addy stopped to read the sign. "Wil-son Bro-thers Gro-cer-y. Eggs forty-eight cents a dozen."

"That's right," Sarah said. "You getting real smart."

"You been a good teacher," Addy said, smiling at her friend. "But you and me not as smart as Harriet. You should see her papers. All 100s. She already doing multiplication."

Sarah didn't say anything. She turned her head to look at a shop window.

"Did you see that blue dress Harriet had on yesterday?" Addy sighed. "It was *so* pretty. I never even seen her in it before. She must have ten or fifteen dresses."

"Let's talk about something else," Sarah cut in. "I don't like talking about her, or even thinking about her."

But Addy liked thinking about Harriet. Harriet had everything that Addy had dreamed freedom would bring *her*. Harriet had fancy dresses. Harriet was smart. Harriet was sure of herself. When they were at their desk together, Harriet helped Addy with her schoolwork. But Harriet never invited Addy to be part of her group. Harriet had many friends. Her friends wore fancy dresses and matching hair ribbons. They buzzed around Harriet as if she were a queen bee. They ate lunch together and played at recess. Addy and Sarah walked home the same way Harriet and her friends did, but Addy and Sarah were never asked to join them.

One day at the end of October, Harriet and her friends were walking home just ahead of Addy and Sarah. Addy started walking faster.

"What you hurrying up for?" Sarah asked sharply.

Addy whispered back, "Let's catch up with them."

"You can if you want," Sarah answered, "but I ain't walking with them."

"Aw, come on. We all going the same way," Addy said softly, catching hold of Sarah's arm.

"I said I ain't walking with them," Sarah repeated loudly.

Harriet stopped and turned around. "I heard you, Sarah," she snapped. "Nobody *asked* you to walk with us." Harriet smiled a cool smile at Addy. "But *you* can come with us if you want, Addy."

Addy got a warm, excited feeling. She turned to look at Sarah, but Sarah wouldn't look at her. Sarah looked down at her scuffed boots. Addy didn't know what to do. She knew she would hurt Sarah if she went with Harriet.

"Sarah isn't the boss of you," Harriet said in a loud voice as Addy hesitated. "You can walk with us whenever you want, Addy. It's your decision." Harriet gave Sarah a nasty look, and then she and her friends disappeared around the corner.

The Lines
Are Drawn

hat evening, Addy was studying her spelling words as Momma made supper. Momma sprinkled flour on the table and began rolling out a piece of dough. She was making biscuits to go with their supper of black-eyed peas. Addy gathered scraps of dough as Momma began cutting the biscuits.

"One word I been wanting to learn to spell is *family*," Momma said to Addy. "You know how to spell that word yet?"

"I do," Addy answered. She started working the scraps of dough into thin strips and made an F and then an A. "Momma, what you think Esther doing right now?" Addy asked as she continued making the letters.

"I suspect she getting ready to eat her supper, too," Momma said.

"I miss her," Addy said, "and Poppa and Sam." She sighed deeply. "Momma, when we gonna live together again like a real family?"

Momma sighed, too. "I can't say when we'll be together again, Addy," she said. "But I don't want you thinking that we ain't a family 'cause we ain't all in one place. We just as much a family as we was back in North Carolina."

Addy finished spelling *family* with the dough pieces. "F-A-M-I-L-Y," Momma read. "Family, that's us."

"That's us." Addy smiled softly.

The next day in school, Miss Dunn talked about the war and about the progress the soldiers from the North were making. "It appears that our Union troops are winning the war," she said proudly.

The class cheered.

Miss Dunn went on. "Now, it's important for the Union soldiers to know we support them."

Harriet interrupted. "My mother does volunteer nursing to help wounded colored soldiers," she said importantly. "She says many of the soldiers she sees are missing an arm or a leg."

Some of the children groaned. "I'm sure that's true," Miss Dunn said. "This has been a very bloody war. The soldiers who make it back alive are lucky, even those who are missing limbs. Many soldiers are dying in battle. All of the men who go off to fight for the North are our heroes. They need to know we care about them. That's why the whole school is going to the Baltimore Depot today to help send off a troop of colored soldiers."

An excited buzz went through the room.

"I wish I was old enough to fight," Billy Maples blurted out. "Even if I lost a leg, I'd still be a hero."

Sarah raised her hand. "Miss Dunn, why there got to be a war at all?" she asked.

Miss Dunn paused for a moment. "Sometimes people fight even when they don't want to. They fight for what they believe is right," she said.

"I still wish there wasn't no war," Sarah said.

Before Miss Dunn could respond to her, Harriet turned around in her seat and said to Sarah, "You know the war is going to free the slaves. You should be glad for the war. *You* were a slave yourself."

"Harriet, that will be enough," Miss Dunn said. "Almost all of us colored people used to be slaves."

"Not me. My family has always been free," Harriet said proudly.

Addy could see a tense look come over Miss Dunn's face.

"Girls and boys, almost all colored people came to America as slaves," she said. "If you weren't a slave, someone in your family probably was. One of the reasons there is a war now is because a line exists between colored and white people. That line is slavery." Miss Dunn turned and faced Harriet. "We don't need to do or say anything that draws more lines between people. The entire country has been divided in two. Let's not make differences based on who was a slave or wasn't, or *anything* else. Is that clear, class?"

"Yes, Miss Dunn," came the answer from all the students together.

"Harriet," Miss Dunn said sharply, "do I make myself clear?"

"Yes, ma'am," Harriet mumbled, embarrassed.

"Good," said Miss Dunn. "When we go to the depot, I want you all to be on your best behavior.

Now line up with your desk partners."

As the class left the building, Harriet put her arm around Addy's shoulders. "So what did you decide?" Harriet asked. "Are you walking home with me and my friends today after school, or do you have to ask Sarah's permission?"

"I don't have to ask her permission," Addy said quickly. "I'm gonna walk with you."

"Good," Harriet said. She sounded satisfied.

By the time the students arrived at the railroad station, a crowd had gathered. The students lined up along the street with the other people to watch the soldiers march by straight and tall in their blue uniforms trimmed with brass buttons. Addy and her class cheered and applauded, but as Addy looked around, she saw that not everyone was cheering. Some women and children were crying as they watched the soldiers march off to war. Then Addy saw one soldier who looked like her brother Sam. Suddenly she felt like crying herself. Addy turned to Harriet and said, "My brother wanted to fight in the war."

"Really?" replied Harriet. She didn't sound interested. "My uncle is serving with the Third Infantry.

That was the first colored regiment organized in the state."

"Oh," said Addy. She wished she knew as much about where Sam was as Harriet knew about her uncle.

On the way back to school, the boys marched straight and tall just as the soldiers had, and the class sang "Rally 'Round the Flag."

When school ended that day, Addy gathered her lunch pail and books and went to Sarah's desk. "I'm gonna walk with Harriet today," Addy said firmly. "She asked me. You can come too if you want."

"No, I can't," Sarah said, her voice shaking.

Addy could see that Sarah was hurt. She was starting to say something to Sarah when she heard Harriet call, "Come on, Addy." Addy turned to see Harriet surrounded by her friends. She gestured for Addy to come.

"Go on," Sarah said bitterly. "You know you want to."

Without looking at Sarah, Addy ran to join Harriet. Once she caught up with Harriet and her friends, she glanced back at Sarah, who was alone. Addy felt torn, but Harriet distracted her.

"How do you think you'll do in the spelling match on Friday?" Harriet asked Addy.

"I hope I'm gonna do all right," Addy replied. "I been studying real hard."

"Can you believe Miss Dunn gave us seventy-five words to learn?" asked Mavis, one of Harriet's friends. She was a tall girl with sandy brown hair.

"Harriet is going to win," another girl said. "She doesn't even have to study."

Addy looked back over her shoulder again for Sarah. But Sarah had disappeared.

"We've been going to my house after school to study for the spelling match," Harriet said. "Maybe you can come with us sometime, Addy. Here." Harriet handed Addy her books. One by one, the other girls piled their books on top.

"These are kinda heavy," Addy said. "Why I got to carry them all?"

"Well, if you want to be with us, you have to be our flunky," Harriet said.

"What's that?" Addy asked, struggling with the books.

Harriet and her friends giggled.

"Oh, Addy, I can tell that you just got off the plantation," said Harriet.

She cast a sly look at Mavis and then said to Addy, "You have to be a flunky because you are the new girl. It's sort of like you have to pass a test to be friends with us."

"What kinda test?" Addy asked.

"Oh, I can't tell you too much. That would be cheating," Harriet said.

The girls all laughed again, and Addy felt too embarrassed to ask more. She felt that the girls all had a secret that they weren't sharing with her.

When the group reached Mrs. Ford's shop, the girls quickly took their books off Addy's pile.

"I'll see y'all tomorrow," Addy called as they walked away.

"Bye," Harriet called, not bothering to look back at Addy.

Inside the shop, Momma and Mrs. Ford were busily working.

"Good afternoon, Mrs. Ford," Addy said. "I know this is a place of business, but can I talk to Momma for a minute?"

"Make it quick," Mrs. Ford said, never looking up from her work.

"Momma, can I go to Harriet's house to study for the spelling match?" Addy asked. "I told you about her before. She my desk partner, and she invited me."

"I suppose it'd be fine," Momma answered, "but only if Sarah go with you."

Addy suddenly felt sick to her stomach. Harriet would never include her if Sarah had to come along.

"Where is your friend?" Mrs. Ford asked.

Addy looked away. "She ain't want to walk with me today," she said.

"That don't sound like Sarah," Momma said.

"It's true, Momma," Addy said quickly. "Anyhow, I know my way around now."

As Addy slowly climbed the long stairs to the garret, she tried to convince herself that what she had just told Momma *was* true. Sarah had *not* wanted to walk with her today. She also tried to figure out a way she could go to Harriet's without Sarah. Addy knew a line had been drawn between Sarah and Harriet and neither one would cross it.

The Spelling Match

he next morning, Addy and Sarah walked most of the way to school in silence. Finally Addy asked, "You angry with me?"

"I ain't angry," Sarah said.

They walked the rest of the way to school without talking. As soon as they arrived, Addy hurried to her desk. Harriet was already sitting there.

"My momma say I could come to your house to study," Addy said happily.

"Really," Harriet said. She sounded cool. "I'm sure you have lots of studying left to do, but I don't really need to study anymore."

"I been studying real hard," Addy said. "We could help each other."

"Well, maybe," Harriet said.

All day Addy felt jumpy with excitement. She

couldn't keep her mind on her work. She kept thinking about the fine house Harriet must have, filled with dolls and other toys. Maybe Harriet would let her play with them this afternoon.

When the day was finally over, Sarah came up to Addy. "You ready to walk home?" she asked.

"Well . . . I'm walking with Harriet," Addy said. "I'm going to her house."

"Fine," Sarah said flatly. "Go with her. I don't care." Her voice did not waver this time. She turned away from Addy.

"Sarah," Addy began. But Harriet's friends surrounded her. The girls dumped their books in Addy's arms again. They were every bit as heavy as the water bucket she used to carry back on the plantation. But Addy didn't complain. At last, she was going to Harriet's house.

"Did you see Sarah today?" Harriet said in a mean voice. "Her dress was so wrinkled, it looked like she slept in it."

Mavis added, "And she had a big brown stain on the front of it."

"Her mother is a washerwoman, and she can't even

keep Sarah's clothes clean," said Harriet.

All the girls laughed, except Addy. "That's not funny," she said. "Her momma work hard."

"She must not be working hard enough, because Sarah is a mess," Harriet said.

"That don't matter," Addy said softly.

Harriet said, "Of course it matters. Anyway, what do you care about Sarah, Addy? You're on our side now. At least your mother keeps you looking present-able, even if you do wear that same old dress every day. Don't you have any others?"

"No," Addy said, swallowing hard.

"Addy looks good enough to be our flunky, though," Mavis said.

The girls all giggled. "That's true," Harriet said lightly. "Sarah didn't. But you, Addy, are a perfect flunky."

Addy smiled weakly, but she had a sick feeling in her stomach.

When the girls reached Mrs. Ford's shop, Harriet suddenly took her books from the pile Addy was carrying. Addy was confused. "Hey, I can go with y'all today," she said. "I can study at your house, Harriet."

"I don't think so. Not today," Harriet said.

"But the spelling match is tomorrow," Addy protested.

Harriet shrugged, "Well, maybe you can come someday, but not today," she repeated. "Come on," she said to the other girls. They grabbed their books and hurried away, leaving Addy alone at the shop door.

Addy stood there, unable to move. Finally, she ran up to the garret and threw herself on the bed. Her face burned as if she had been stung by a swarm of bees. Sarah had been right. Harriet did not want Addy to be her friend. She just wanted Addy to be her slave. And even worse, Addy had chosen to be her slave. Addy reached for the cowrie shell Momma had given her and cried with shame.

The next day was the day of the spelling match. When Addy woke up, Momma was already at the stove stirring a pot of grits. Addy got up and washed in a small basin beside the bed. She looked for the dress that Momma always laid out over the back of her chair, but her dress wasn't there. In its place were a new blue skirt and jacket trimmed in black braid and a crisp white shirt. Addy stood staring at them.

"I made them out of some leftover cloth from the shop. I want you to look your best for that spelling match," Momma said, smiling. "You surprised?"

"Oh, Momma, thank you," Addy said, throwing her arms around Momma. "They nicer than anything I ever dreamed about."

Momma took the clothes off the chair and helped Addy dress. "I been staying up late for weeks now working on them, hoping I could surprise you," said Momma, fastening the skirt. When Momma stood back to admire Addy in her new clothes, her dark eyes sparkled with pride. "Look at you! You look like a fancy city girl," Momma said. "No matter how you do in the spelling match, I'm gonna be proud of you. You done worked real hard."

But as Addy walked to school that morning in her new outfit, she didn't feel she deserved the new clothes. Once she got to school, the hours dragged by slowly. Addy became more and more nervous during the morning lessons. When the spelling match finally started, her stomach felt queasy.

Harriet was given the first word to spell—*carriage*. She rattled off the letters quickly, "C-A-R-R-I-A-G-E."

"Correct," Miss Dunn said. "Sarah, you have the next word. Spell *button*."

"B-U-T-T-O-N," Sarah spelled in a soft voice.

"Correct," said Miss Dunn. "Addy, it's your turn. Spell *tomorrow*."

Addy started to spell quickly, just as Harriet had. "T-O-M-O-R-O-," but then she stopped. This was one of the words she had trouble spelling. She stopped and thought. She knew she could spell this word. She started again, this time more slowly, "T-O-M-O-R-R-O-W."

"Correct," Miss Dunn said.

Addy breathed a sigh of relief. At least she wouldn't make a mistake in the first round of the spelling match.

Harriet leaned over and whispered, "I'm going to win, and my mother said I can have friends over after school for ice cream to celebrate. She said I could bring five girls. I might ask you."

Addy said nothing. Her stomach felt worse.

After two rounds, half the class had missed a spelling word and had to sit down. Addy was glad that Sarah was still in the contest.

Sarah's next word was *account.*

Sarah began, "A-C-C-," and then she paused.

Addy closed her eyes. *O-U-N-T,* she thought. *Come on, Sarah, you can spell it. A-C-C-O-U-N-T.*

Sarah began again, "A-C-C-O-N-T," she said.

"I'm sorry," Miss Dunn said. "That's not correct."

Addy's turn was next. She took a deep breath. She knew how to spell the word, but she didn't want to hurt Sarah any more. She decided she would spell it wrong on purpose to apologize to Sarah.

But before Miss Dunn called on Addy, Harriet whispered to her again. "I can't believe Sarah missed such an easy one," she said. "She is so dumb."

Addy felt a flash of anger. *I'll show her,* Addy thought. When Miss Dunn called on her, Addy spelled the word correctly.

The spelling match went into the third round. Addy spelled *bridge* correctly. In the fourth round, she got *scissors* right. When the fifth round came, there were two spellers left: Harriet and Addy.

Harriet had the first word. "*Principle,*" Miss Dunn said. "We all live our lives by principles. *Principle.*"

"P-R-I-N-S-I-P-L-E," Harriet said quickly.

"I'm sorry," Miss Dunn said. "That is not correct."

The students started talking among themselves.

"Quiet," Miss Dunn demanded. "Give Addy a chance to think in peace. Addy, you must spell the word correctly to win. Principle."

Slowly and deliberately, Addy spelled out the letters, "P-R-I-N-C-I-P-L-E."

"Correct!" Miss Dunn exclaimed. She beamed with delight as she said, "Addy Walker, you have truly earned this prize."

Miss Dunn came over to Addy and pinned a medal on her jacket. "Your hard work has paid off," she said. "Class, please clap for Addy." The boys and girls clapped and cheered. It was time for lunch by then, and Miss Dunn announced that the class could eat outside because it was a warm day. Several girls rushed up to Addy to congratulate her before they left the classroom.

Harriet stood at the edge of the group. "Well," she said briskly. "If I had studied at all, I would have beaten you. Anyway, Miss Dunn gave you easier words."

"You're just jealous, Harriet," Mavis said. "Addy spelled the word *you* missed."

"I'm not jealous of her," Harriet shrugged.

But Mavis was saying to Addy, "You have on such a pretty new outfit. Where did your mother buy it?"

"She ain't buy it, she made it," Addy answered.

"It's so nice," Mavis said, touching the braid on the jacket. "I wish my mother could sew like this."

Harriet cut into the conversation. "We're eating out on the front steps if you want to join us," she said to Addy. "Come on, girls."

Addy watched as Harriet and her friends went outside. Then she sat down at her desk, pretending she was looking for something inside it. She felt a hand on her shoulder. It was Miss Dunn.

"This is a very special day for you, Addy. Why are you in here all by yourself?" the teacher asked.

Addy kept rooting through her desk.

"I don't think you'll find what you're looking for inside that desk, Addy," Miss Dunn said.

Addy still did not look up.

Miss Dunn reached for Addy's hand. "Addy, look at me," she said gently. Addy slowly looked up. "I suspect you're feeling bad because lines have been drawn between some girls in this class."

"Miss Dunn," Addy said, "I don't know how to get

rid of the lines. I done hurt Sarah, and I wouldn't blame her if she never spoke to me again."

"We all make mistakes," Miss Dunn said. "I suspect you've learned a lesson about friendship. But you can't make things better by hiding in here. You need to think about what you stand for and act on it." Miss Dunn smiled at Addy and then left her alone.

Addy took her lunch pail from the floor, opened the lid, and looked to see what Momma had packed. When she saw what was on top, she closed the lid and hurried out of the classroom. Addy went around to the side of the building. She stopped when she saw Sarah sitting alone under a small tree. Addy took a deep breath. Then she walked up to Sarah and knelt beside her.

"I'm so sorry, Sarah," Addy said. "Please forgive me. I wanted to be friends with Harriet because she was popular and smart and rich. But she ain't a real friend. I know you is. I never meant to hurt you. I want you to still be my friend."

"I still want to be your friend," Sarah said, smiling that sunny smile Addy had seen the first day she and Momma had arrived at the pier. Then Sarah reached out and touched Addy's medal.

"I wanted you to win so bad," Sarah said.

"I wanted you to win, too. I was sad when you missed your word," Addy said. "Maybe we can study spelling together right now." She reached into her lunch pail. There on top were four cookies Momma had made, each in the shape of a letter. L-O-V-E.

"Here," Addy said, holding the cookies on her outstretched hand. "This is our first word."

Winds of
Winter

ddy knew that winter had come to Philadelphia even before she opened her eyes. It was late November, and an icy wind whistled through the crack in the garret window. Momma had just gotten up, letting a puff of cold air in the bed when she lifted the heavy quilt. But her place was still warm, so Addy snuggled into it.

Momma's gentle voice called to her. "Addy, honey, I need your help over here. Snow's coming right in through the window."

Addy peeked out from under the quilt. In the dim gray light of morning, she saw Momma straining to close the window. Its panes were white with frost. A little pile of snow had built up on the windowsill, and more snow had blown across the floor. "I'm coming, Momma," she said.

Addy crawled out of bed and shivered over to the window to help Momma. Together they pulled down on the window, struggling to close it. But the window wouldn't budge.

"Go get them rags next to the stove," Momma said.

Addy got the rags and returned to Momma.

"Help me stuff these in the crack, Addy," said Momma as she poked the rags between the window and the sill. "Stuff them good. They all we got to keep the wind from coming in."

Addy put one cold foot on top of the other to try to warm up her feet. "Can't we light the stove this morning, Momma?" she asked. "It's so cold in here."

"No, honey," Momma said. "We got just enough coal to last us the week if we use it only for cooking supper." She smiled at Addy and gave her a quick, warm hug. "Now you wash up and get ready for school. And hustle, you hear? Then you won't feel the cold so bad."

Addy splashed icy cold water from the basin over her face and dressed quickly, dancing around in her stocking feet. She waited to pull on her boots until the very end. They were still wet from the puddle she had

stepped in on her way home from school yesterday.
Though she had set them by the stove last night, the
fire hadn't been warm long enough to dry them out.

Addy wrapped her shawl around her shoulders and
sat down at the table to eat the cornbread Momma had
set out for her. She crumbled it in a bowl and poured
buttermilk over it. As she ate, she spied a pile of fabric
folded neatly on Momma's chair, with a spool of thread
and a pair of scissors on top.

"You was up late again sewing, Momma, wasn't
you?" asked Addy.

"I got to finish this dress for Mrs. Howell," Momma
answered. "Mrs. Ford say Mrs. Howell is real particu-
lar." Momma unfolded the fabric and squinted at one of
the seams she had sewn last night. "It's hard to see my
stitches by candlelight. We sure do need a lamp."

"How much we got saved for it?" asked Addy. "Can
I count up the money in the milk bottle again?"

Momma nodded. "Sure you can," she said, "but
I ain't put nothing in since you counted it last week."

"I put my tips in last Saturday, Momma," Addy
said proudly. "I got two big tips when I delivered them
dresses to Society Hill for Mrs. Ford."

"That's good, Addy," said Momma. She reached into their hiding place behind the stove, picked up the milk bottle, and handed it to Addy. Addy turned the bottle upside down and shook it so that the coins poured out. Then she carefully counted the pennies, half dimes, and dimes.

"We got one dollar and fifty-seven cents," Addy announced.

"Well, that ain't enough for a lamp," said Momma. "Guess we gonna have to wait a little longer. Just hope I don't have to pull them stitches out of one of them seams in that dress."

Addy finished her breakfast and washed her bowl and spoon in the bucket of water that stood by the stove. Then she sat back down so Momma could brush and braid her hair. She looked at the thick folds of green and red plaid taffeta that lay over the chair next to her.

"Them rich girls sure got pretty dresses," said Addy.

"Sure do," said Momma. "Isabella Howell's gonna wear that one to some fancy Christmas party."

"Remember last Christmas, Momma?" asked Addy.

She thought back to last year when she and Momma were on the plantation with Poppa, Sam, and Esther. "Master Stevens gave us a real skinny chicken. Sam wouldn't even eat it after you cooked it. He was mad because of how hard we worked. He said one chicken couldn't make up for a whole year of work. But I was hungry, and I ate it."

"I remember," Momma said, "but Sam ate my sweet-potato pudding. He liked that."

"And Poppa did, too," Addy said. "Sweet-potato pudding was Poppa's favorite. He always said so. He always . . ." Addy stopped. She missed Poppa and Sam and Esther so much.

Momma seemed to know just what Addy was feeling. As she started to braid Addy's hair, she said, "I'm gonna make that pudding for Christmas again this year. We'll take it to the church dinner. Auntie Lula taught me to make it. I'm sure she gonna be making it this year, too. So when we have Christmas dinner, we'll be eating the same thing as Auntie Lula, Uncle Solomon, and Esther."

"I wonder what Esther's Christmas is gonna be like," worried Addy.

"Well, Auntie Lula and Uncle Solomon ain't gonna have to work on Christmas, so they can be with her all day long," said Momma. She finished Addy's first braid and started on the second one. "And you left your doll Janie with her. That's like Esther having a present to play with every day."

"Last night I dreamed we was all together. Sam, Poppa, Esther—all of us here in Philadelphia," said Addy. She turned her head to look at Momma, who looked sad. Momma gently turned Addy's head back and continued braiding.

"It ain't gonna be just a dream, Momma. It's really gonna happen someday, ain't it?" Addy asked hopefully. "Ain't we all gonna be together someday?"

"Someday, honey. Someday. That dream keep me going. That and your bright face." Momma finished the second braid and leaned over to kiss the top of Addy's head.

On the way to school that morning, Addy asked Sarah what Christmas was like in freedom. Sarah described the celebration at church.

"I hope it's gonna be just like last year," said Sarah. "The altar was all decorated with pine branches. In the middle was a manger with baby Jesus, and Mary and Joseph kneeling next to it. There was three wise men and a bunch of angels and even a silvery star hanging from the ceiling. Lots of candles was on the altar. The whole church was glowing and beautiful. I'm telling you, Addy, it's the prettiest thing you'll ever see. Ever."

Addy could barely imagine something so lovely.

Sarah went on, "After the service, we go downstairs for the big Christmas dinner. Everybody bring something to share and everyone in the whole church sit down like one great big family."

"Momma said we was gonna bring sweet-potato pudding, just like we had last year for Christmas," said Addy.

"Mmm, that sound good," said Sarah brightly, "but I ain't told you the best part yet, Addy. After dinner, there's a special shadow play for children."

"What's that?" asked Addy.

"Well, it's kind of hard to describe," said Sarah. "We sit in a dark room that has this big sheet hanging in the front. Behind it, there's this bright lamp. People in front of the lamp make shadows on the sheet. They act out the Christmas story while it's read out loud."

"I bet it's real nice," Addy said.

"You gonna love it," Sarah said excitedly. "And this year my momma's letting me sing in the children's choir. You should join, too. We practice every Saturday till Christmas."

"I wish I could, but I can't," said Addy. "Saturday is when I work for Mrs. Ford. I'm doing errands and deliveries so she and Momma can spend all their time sewing Christmas dresses for the customers. Mrs. Ford let me keep the tips from the deliveries. I had to promise I would keep up with my lessons."

"What are you going to do with your money?" asked Sarah.

"Momma and me saving for a lamp," answered Addy. "Maybe by the time I finish all the Christmas deliveries, we might have enough saved up."

"Well, don't worry, Addy," said Sarah kindly. "If you can't come to choir practice, I'll teach you the songs. Then you can sing on Christmas along with everyone else."

"I'd like that," said Addy. She smiled at her friend.

"We can start right now," said Sarah. "The first song we always sing is 'Joy to the World.' Here's how it goes." With that, Sarah began to sing. Addy listened and then hummed along. Soon she knew the words.

"Joy to the world!" the two girls sang together as they hurried through the winter streets to school.

Something
Pretty

arly on Saturday morning, Addy set out on
her errands and deliveries for Mrs. Ford. She
brought a bill to a customer on Society Hill.
Then she went to the dry goods store a few blocks away
to pick up supplies that Mrs. Ford had ordered. The
thread, buttons, ribbon, and fringe were wrapped into
one parcel before Addy left the store.

Addy held on to her parcel tightly as she stepped
around the slush and dirty puddles in the streets. On
the way to her next stop, she passed the windows of
Mr. Delmonte's Secondhand Shop. Sometimes she and
Momma went there to look for clothes or pots and
pans. The socks Addy had on today had come from
Mr. Delmonte's. There was a small darn in the heel of
one sock, but the other was as good as new.

Addy stopped for a minute to look in the window.

Lying among the used shoes, wool caps, and old belts was a bright patch of red cloth. It looked like the corner of a scarf, but most of it was hidden behind a rusty tea kettle. Addy went inside to take a closer look.

Mr. Delmonte recognized her right away. "Good morning, Addy," he said in his jolly way. "What brings you here today?"

"Can I see that red scarf in the window?" Addy asked.

Mr. Delmonte reached into the window display and moved the tea kettle so he could lift out the scarf and hand it to Addy. "It's a beauty," he said. "Hardly looks worn."

Addy unfolded the scarf. It was like new. The red fabric was soft and smooth. Addy held it up to her cheek. Right then she knew she wanted Momma to have the scarf. *Momma should have something pretty like this,* thought Addy. *She work so hard. She'd look so beautiful in this when we go to the Christmas service at church.* Addy was almost afraid to ask about the price, but she looked up at Mr. Delmonte.

"How much it cost?" she asked.

"Twenty cents," answered Mr. Delmonte. "It's a

good price for something that looks like it's never been worn."

Addy was discouraged. She didn't have twenty cents. But she had to buy that scarf somehow.

"Please, Mr. Delmonte," she said, "could you put it away for me? I'm gonna try my best to get the money to buy it."

"Well, I'll put it back behind that rusty kettle again," answered Mr. Delmonte. "You're the only person who's spotted it since I put it in the window last week. It'll probably stay there a little longer."

"I hope so," said Addy as she carefully folded the scarf and handed it back to Mr. Delmonte.

The feel of the soft material and its bright red color stayed in Addy's mind as she headed back to Mrs. Ford's shop. *How am I gonna get twenty cents?* she wondered.

Back at the shop, Mrs. Ford had three packages for her to deliver, all wrapped in brown paper. "These go to Society Hill," said Mrs. Ford as she handed them to Addy. "Be careful. Don't splash mud on them."

"Yes, ma'am," said Addy.

The streets were busier that afternoon than they were in the morning. Addy had to dodge around throngs of people bustling in and out of shops. Her packages were clumsy, and she worried about dropping them on the sloppy sidewalks. After Momma had worked so hard, Addy wanted to make sure the dresses were delivered in perfect condition. The last delivery was on Spruce Street. As Addy walked toward the address, she saw an old man lighting the street lamps. The lamps cast a golden glow on the wet sidewalks. When Addy got to the house, she rang the bell and waited for the big door to open. A maid finally came, and Addy handed her the last bundle.

"This is from Mrs. Ford's shop," she said proudly.

The maid took the package and handed Addy five pennies. Addy thanked her and turned away. As she walked back down Spruce Street, she curled her fingers around the coins inside her mitten.

Suddenly, Addy had an idea. She decided to stop by Mr. Delmonte's shop again on the way home, just to be sure the soft red scarf was still there. As she approached the store, Mr. Delmonte was just locking up.

"Don't worry, Addy," he said. "The scarf is still here. I moved it off in the corner a bit, but you can see it if you know where to look."

The two of them stood at the window together. Mr. Delmonte headed down the street, but Addy stayed at the window, thinking about her idea. *If I put half my tips in the milk bottle,* she thought, *and keep the other half, maybe I can save enough money to buy the scarf for Momma!* Addy lingered a little longer, staring at the scarf in the fading light, thinking how pretty Momma would look in it. Then she headed back to Mrs. Ford's shop.

By the time she got to the shop, her feet were numb with cold and her nose felt frozen.

"You look frozen stiff, child," said Mrs. Ford, peering above her spectacles. Mrs. Ford had a tape measure draped around her neck. Momma had a ribbon thrown across one shoulder as she sewed fringe on the end of a sash. They looked busy, and Addy knew she shouldn't bother them.

"Momma, can I light the stove upstairs now?" asked Addy. "Please?"

"No, Addy," Momma answered. "You know we don't light the stove until I start cooking supper. You head on upstairs. I'll be up as soon as I finish this sash. Then we'll light the stove."

"Yes, Momma," said Addy.

As she headed out the door, she heard Mrs. Ford ask Momma, "How is everything up in the garret?"

"Everything is fine," Momma answered quickly. "We get by."

Addy wanted to turn around and tell Mrs. Ford the truth, that it was freezing in the garret, and dark, and sometimes very lonely. On the plantation, Addy had been allowed to spend more time with Momma than she was here. She wanted to tell Mrs. Ford about the broken window and the snow on the floor. But Addy knew Momma would not want her to complain.

"We get by," Addy said softly to herself as she climbed the stairs.

When she got to the top, she lit the candle on the table. Addy turned her mitten upside down and let her tip money fall onto the table. She brought the milk bottle out from behind the stove and set it next to the money. Then Addy went over to the bed and lifted up a corner of the mattress. There she found the kerchief that she had brought from the plantation when she and Momma had escaped from slavery. Tied in one corner was the half dime Uncle Solomon had given her. It was the only money they had when they headed north for freedom. "Freedom's got its cost," Uncle Solomon had said when he gave it to Addy. She had saved it for something very special, something important.

Addy brought the kerchief over to the table and divided her tip money into two piles. She dropped one pile into the milk bottle and then carefully tied the other coins into the corner of her kerchief. With Uncle Solomon's half dime, she had ten cents in the kerchief. That was half of what she needed for Momma's red scarf. *I'm halfway there!* Addy thought to herself. The thought made her so happy, she didn't think about the cold.

Freedom Ain't Free

t church the next morning, Momma and Addy sat side by side in the women's section. Addy looked across the aisle where all the men sat and imagined that someday her poppa would be sitting over there, smiling and giving her a wink that said, "You my favorite girl."

When the deep notes of the organ sounded, everyone stood to sing. The first song was one of Addy's favorites. Auntie Lula had taught it to her back on the plantation. Now Addy sang out with the others in joy.

> *This little light of mine,*
> *I'm gonna let it shine,*
> *Let it shine, let it shine, let it shine.*

After a long prayer, Reverend Drake began his sermon. "I want to begin this morning by reading from the Book of Luke. Turn to chapter two, verses six and seven."

Momma took a Bible from the rack on the pew in front of them. Addy helped her find the passage.

Reverend Drake said, "This passage I'm about to read to you is about Mary and Joseph."

Addy and Momma and the other members followed along as Reverend Drake read: "'And she brought forth her firstborn son, and wrapped him in swaddling clothes, and laid him in a manger because there was no room for them in the inn.'

"Now, this is the story of Christmas, the story of the birth of Jesus. The time had come for Mary to give birth to Jesus. Let me tell you people, time is a curious thing. It can't be stopped like a clock," Reverend Drake said.

"You right, Reverend," one church member called out.

"Time keeps right on moving. And I'm here to tell you the *time* for freedom has come for thousands of our people. These freedmen are waiting right now in Washington, D.C., and other cities. And they need our help. Stay with me, now," Reverend Drake preached. "Think with me. Because I'm here to tell you this morning, freedom ain't free!"

A church member shouted back, "You preaching the truth!"

Addy scooted over closer to Momma and laid her head on Momma's shoulder. Momma put her arm around Addy and rocked gently on the pew. Addy liked coming to church. Anyone who wanted to could take part in the service. If you felt like answering the reverend, you could. If you felt like crying, or laughing, or clapping to the music the choir sang, you could.

Reverend Drake continued, "Some of you already know what I'm talking about because there was a *time* when you came to freedom, and you found out what freedom was about. It wasn't free! You needed food to eat, clothes to wear, a place to stay."

"Amen!" Momma replied.

"I'm here to tell you people, time ain't gonna stop for those thousands of freedmen who need our help. As I speak to you, babies are being born, and children are hungry, and mothers and fathers have no place to lay their heads at night. They need our help now, today!" Reverend Drake said, his voice getting louder.

Addy looked up at Momma and saw tears running down her face. Addy gave Momma a little hug.

"As we enter the season of Advent, the time of preparing for Christmas, let God work through you. When the collection boxes are passed this morning, remember to put in a little extra for our Freedmen's Fund. These people are your cousins, your brothers and sisters, your mothers and fathers," Reverend Drake said, pounding on the pulpit.

"It might mean you have to sacrifice. If you can't give of your money, give of your time. Next Saturday a group of freedmen are coming in at the pier. Come help us welcome them to freedom.

"I close by saying, freedom can be a lonely walk through the wilderness and dark. But you can make a difference between a lonely night and one filled with light and hope!"

On the way home from church, Momma and Addy walked hand in hand, humming "This Little Light of Mine." Even though it was cold out, Addy felt a warm glow inside.

"I been thinking about what Reverend Drake said

this morning," said Momma slowly. "He made me remember how it was for you and me when we first came to Philadelphia. We had nothing. The church helped us when we needed it. Now we done saved more than a dollar fifty. The freedmen need our help right now. They need our savings more than we do. We can get along without a lamp, but they can't get along without help. What do you think?"

At first, Addy did not say anything. It was true. She and Momma could get along without the lamp. But they had saved so hard for it. A lamp would help her see better when she did her homework, and it would help Momma when she had to sew late at night. Addy could imagine how nice it would be to have a lamp when Sam and Poppa and Esther returned, when their family was at last together again. She could picture their faces glowing in the bright light as they gathered around the dinner table. But then she remembered how scared and lonely she and Momma had been when they first came to Philadelphia, and how the church had helped them find work, a place to live, and friends.

"I think we should give our money to the church,"

Addy said. "Other people helped us. The money might even help Sam or Poppa or Esther come to us."

"Even if it don't," replied Momma, "it's gonna help *somebody*. That's what's important." She squeezed Addy's hand. "We'll give the church our money next Sunday."

With a pang of guilt, Addy remembered the ten cents she had knotted up in her kerchief. Should she give that to help the freedmen, too? *No,* thought Addy. *I can't give that money away. It's for Momma's Christmas surprise.* Addy decided to keep the money. She was determined to buy the scarf and show Momma how much she loved her. She would find another way to help the freedmen. "Momma," she asked, "can I go to the pier next Saturday to help out with the freedmen?"

"I think that would be fine, Addy," said Momma, "just so you finish all of Mrs. Ford's deliveries."

"I will, Momma," Addy promised.

The Cost of
Freedom

hen Addy arrived at the pier the next Saturday, Reverend Drake was already handing out old clothes and blankets to the people who had just gotten off the boat. Sarah and her mother were there, just as they had been when Addy and Momma arrived in Philadelphia last summer. Addy was glad to see them.

"What am I supposed to say to these folks?" Addy asked Sarah.

"You ain't got to say nothing special," Sarah said. "Just be yourself."

"I wish I could be like you," Addy said. "When you met us, you made me feel like I was coming home."

"I was scared the day I met you," Sarah admitted, "and look how good things turned out for us."

The pier was slick with mud. Garbage floated in the

dark, icy water, and the newly freed people huddled together in silent groups. They looked cold, frightened, hungry, and lost. Addy closed her eyes for a second. *Esther. Sam. Poppa. Be here. Be here,* Addy wished. But when she opened her eyes, there were no familiar faces in the crowd. Addy's heart sank.

Just then she saw a thin woman who held a bundle in her arms. Addy heard a sharp cry. For a second, Addy thought it was Esther crying, and her heart started to pound. Then she saw a little hand reach up from the bundle. Quickly, Addy pulled her shawl from around her shoulders and handed it to the woman, who thanked her and wrapped the shawl around her baby.

Addy held out her arms. "I can carry the baby, if you like," she said. "I'll be careful."

The woman smiled weakly. "Thank you kindly," she said. She handed the baby to Addy. Addy cradled the baby in her arms just as she used to cradle Esther. The baby's eyes were bright as buttons. Addy held the baby close to her chest, hoping to warm her. The baby waved her arms and grabbed the cowrie shell necklace Addy wore around her neck. The baby's mother smiled.

"She like you," she said. "She don't take a shine to just anybody."

The woman rode back to the church in the wagon that Reverend Drake had brought, along with an old man who was coughing so hard his whole body shook. Another man in the wagon had been limping along with a stick he used as a crutch. His foot was bandaged in dirty rags. Addy looked at the poor, tired people who plodded along behind the wagon. Some had no shoes. Others wore tattered clothes. Addy held the baby closer to her, trying to keep her warm.

"Where y'all from?" Addy asked the baby's mother.

"We coming up from Baltimore," said the woman. "All the slaves on our plantation was turned out about a month ago. We was told we was free and we had to get. But we ain't had nowhere to go. No food. No nothing. Me and some others walked together. For a week, we ate almost nothing but grass. We walked until we got to Baltimore."

"Things gonna be better here," promised Addy. "The people at the church helped me and my momma. They'll help you, too."

When the wagon arrived back at church, Addy led

the woman to Fellowship Hall in the basement. The
big room was warm and dry and filled with the smell
of delicious food. Many church members were there
to help serve food to the freedmen. Addy remembered how happy she and Momma had been in this
same place, eating their first warm meal in freedom
on their first day in Philadelphia. She said good-bye
to the woman. "You be safe now," she said. "People in
the church gonna be your family." Addy hugged the
baby one last time. Memories of Esther filled her mind,
and she squeezed her eyes tight to stop the tears. Then
Addy left to go to Mrs. Ford's.

Back at the shop, there were more errands to do and
three deliveries to make. Addy hurried along the busy
streets. She saw women in fancy hats and fur coats carrying packages wrapped in bright paper. Usually Addy
would have been fascinated with their fine clothes
and fancy manners, but today they seemed silly. She
remembered the people shivering at the pier. A man
in a top hat strolled by, swinging a fine walking stick.
Addy thought of the man at the pier with his foot in
dirty bandages. When Addy made a delivery to one of
the biggest houses on Society Hill, all she could think

of were the freedmen who had arrived that morning. None of them had a place to stay at all.

Addy got tips from the first two houses she went to. The coins jingled in her mitten, and she began to think cheerfully about the scarf that she would soon be able to buy for Momma. If she got a five-cent tip from her last delivery, she would have just enough for the scarf. Addy began to walk faster. Her last delivery was the beautiful plaid dress for Isabella Howell. It was the dress Momma had worked the hardest on, and Addy was very proud to be delivering it. She lifted the shiny brass knocker on the front door and banged it loudly three times.

Soon a woman came. "Who are you?" she asked coldly.

"I'm Addy Walker. This here is a dress from Mrs. Ford's dress shop. It's for Isabella Howell."

"Very well then," said the maid as she took the package. "Wait here."

Addy stood in the entrance of the Howells' mansion. The house looked more beautiful than any house she'd ever seen. A staircase of dark wood curved up to the second floor. Addy could see into the living room, too. She saw a high-backed pink couch and pink chairs. Instead of kerosene lamps, the room had gas lamps, each one lighted and covered by a glass globe. In the corner, a decorated Christmas tree reached up to the ceiling. The lamplight filled the room with a rosy glow, and a fire burned in the hearth.

The maid returned shortly and pressed a coin into Addy's hand. "Here's a tip for you, child. Now run along," she said, hurrying Addy out the door.

Addy was outside. The big door had closed behind her before she looked at the coin in her hand. She couldn't believe what she saw. "A dime!" said Addy out loud. "A whole dime." It was the biggest tip Addy had ever gotten. She slid it into her mitten. Now she had enough for Momma's scarf! She even had a little extra to put in the milk bottle to start saving for the lamp again.

Addy skipped down the walk and ran all the way back to the shop. She didn't even stop in to see Momma and Mrs. Ford. Instead, she ran upstairs and took her kerchief out from under the mattress. She untied the knot and let the coins fall on the table. She turned her mitten upside down and dumped the tips she had made that day into the pile of money. Carefully, she counted twenty cents for Momma's scarf. Then she dropped the rest of the money in the milk bottle. The twenty cents went into her mitten. She would get the scarf this afternoon after she finished her errands. She could hardly wait!

Addy's last chore of the day was to get Mrs. Ford's scissors sharpened. The sharpener's shop was not too far from Mr. Delmonte's shop. If Addy hurried, she could get the scissors sharpened and buy the scarf before it got dark.

The grinding wheel that sharpened the scissors made a loud whining noise, so Addy waited outside. People pushed past her in a hurry to get home. Streetcars clanged and carriages rushed by, but she hardly noticed them. All she could think about was Momma's beautiful scarf and how surprised she would be on Christmas morning.

A woman pushing a fancy baby buggy wheeled toward Addy and stopped in front of the shop. The buggy was too big to fit through the door, so the woman parked it next to Addy and lifted out a little baby all bundled in soft fleecy blankets. The baby started to fuss. Suddenly, Addy remembered the baby she'd held that morning. Then she began to think about Esther. *My sister might not be as lucky as that baby at the pier. Who's gonna give money for her to come to freedom?*

Addy felt the coins she held in her hand inside the mitten. It was only twenty cents. But if everyone gave as much as possible, then all the newly freed people could get to the North—maybe even Esther. Addy stood quietly by herself for a minute, her heart aching with the memory of her baby sister. Then she turned and went inside to pick up the scissors.

Addy headed toward Mr. Delmonte's store. It was still open. She could see the pretty red scarf tucked behind the tea kettle in the window. But Addy didn't go inside. Instead, she walked on down the street for a few more blocks until she came to the church. With both hands, she pulled open the heavy door. She walked over to the box at the side of the church. Above it was a sign that said "Freedmen's Fund." Slowly, Addy took off her mitten. One by one, she dropped her coins into the box. The last coin was the half dime Uncle Solomon had given her. She remembered the words he said to her, "Freedom's got its cost." Then she thought of Esther, Sam, and Poppa, still waiting to take their freedom, and she let the half dime clink into the box with the rest of her money.

When Addy got back to the shop, she could see Momma and Mrs. Ford through the window. They were sitting next to the stove with their heads bent over their sewing. Addy knew that they were working on the last two dresses that had to be done before Christmas. Both women looked up when Addy came through the door.

"There won't be any more deliveries today," said Mrs. Ford.

"You run along now, Addy," said Momma. "I'll be up soon to start supper."

As Addy turned to leave, Mrs. Ford spoke again. "There's no sense in you going upstairs. Stay here with me and your mother."

Addy turned around and looked at Mrs. Ford and then at Momma. She could not believe her ears! Did Mrs. Ford say she could stay in the shop?

Momma said, "Addy will be all right upstairs, Mrs. Ford. I know you running a business here, and you don't want children in the shop."

"I know I've said that in the past," Mrs. Ford said
to Momma, "but I believe that Addy has served my
business well, and I don't think she'll be in the way."

Addy stood at the door with her back against the
knob. She looked at Momma, who looked puzzled.
Addy was puzzled, too. She had no idea what Mrs.
Ford was up to.

"Take this," Mrs. Ford said to Addy. She handed
Addy a needle book with two shiny needles inside.
"While your mother and I are working, you can keep
yourself busy. I know your mother's taught you how to
make a hem. Here is a plain apron you can practice on."

"Oh, thank you, Mrs. Ford," Addy said.

"There's no need to thank me," Mrs. Ford said as
she went back to her sewing.

"Come sit on this crate by me," Momma said.
"I'll keep an eye on your stitches."

Addy sat down next to Momma and spread the
white apron across her lap. She smoothed it out and
then threaded the needle and knotted it tight. She
picked up the corner of the apron and started to sew
the hem. Carefully and slowly, Addy went about her

task. She concentrated hard on her stitches, making them even and straight.

Addy was glad to have a job to do. It helped her get her mind off the scarf. But more than anything, she was glad to be with Momma.

Christmas
Surprises
CHAPTER 15

rom that day on, Addy was allowed to spend her afternoons sewing in the warm shop with Momma and Mrs. Ford instead of in the cold garret by herself. Business had begun to slow down. Momma and Mrs. Ford were just finishing up a few small items.

Four days before Christmas, Addy was straightening up the shop for Mrs. Ford. She loved to sort the buttons into boxes, arrange the feathers according to size, and straighten the creamy laces and loopy fringes. She carefully wound the ribbons back on their spools and organized the thread by color. She folded the beautiful fabrics and piled them neatly on the shelves. By the end of the afternoon, all that was left to do was to pick up the pins that had fallen on the floor in the Christmas bustle.

Addy was on her hands and knees filling the pin box when the door burst open and in stormed an angry woman. Right behind her was a tall, plump girl. Addy knew the woman must be Mrs. Howell because she carried the beautiful green plaid dress that Momma had worked so hard on. She thrust it toward Mrs. Ford.

"Look at this dress," she fumed. "Just look at it!"

Mrs. Ford took the dress and held it up in front of her. The seams on the sides were split open, and the threads of the plaid fabric were frayed. The buttons on the back had popped off. The dress looked wrinkled and droopy, as if someone had tossed it in a heap on the floor.

"This dress was made too small," Mrs. Howell raged. "I've never seen such poor work."

Addy looked at Momma, who kept her eyes on the sewing in her lap. Addy could see Momma's lips tighten in anger.

"Stop right there," Mrs. Ford said firmly. "Ruth Walker here is the best seamstress I've ever had working for me. I am sure the dress was not made too small. It was sewn to the exact measurements we took at the fitting last month. Perhaps Isabella has grown some."

Addy looked at Isabella. She stood near the door, looking at her feet. Her round face flushed pink.

Mrs. Ford went on. "If you are unhappy, I will give you a full refund, Mrs. Howell—not because the dress was poorly made, but because you are dissatisfied."

Mrs. Ford opened the drawer where she kept the money. She reached inside and took out a handful of bills, which she quickly counted into Mrs. Howell's hand. "Now good day to you, madam," Mrs. Ford said coldly as she pushed the drawer shut with a bang.

"Good day!" said Mrs. Howell. A blast of cold air blew into the shop as the door slammed behind them.

Mrs. Ford sat back down. As she picked up her sewing, she said, "I can't believe she acted that way. Some people have no idea what the Christmas season is all about."

As Christmas approached, almost no one came into the shop. All of the dresses had been finished. Addy made her last delivery on the day before Christmas, taking a red hat to a lady on Society Hill. When she returned to the shop in the early afternoon, Momma wasn't there.

"She's gone upstairs for a rest. Your mother's worked hard," said Mrs. Ford. "I plan to close the shop early this afternoon and take a rest myself."

Addy started to head upstairs, but Mrs. Ford stopped her. "Before you go, Addy, I have one last package." She handed a parcel wrapped in brown paper to Addy.

"Who is this for?" Addy asked.

"Open it," said Mrs. Ford. "It's for you."

Addy untied the package and could hardly believe what was inside. It was the green plaid dress Momma had made for Isabella Howell! But it looked like new. All the seams were repaired and the buttons had been replaced.

"I want you to have this dress, Addy," Mrs. Ford said. "You've been such a big help to your mother and me this Christmas season. You have worked hard. I've made the dress smaller to fit you. The hem just needs to be cut to the right length. Slip the dress on now and I'll pin it right up before I leave."

Addy didn't know what to say. She just stared at the dress. "Yes, ma'am," she said.

Addy stood on a crate while Mrs. Ford kneeled on the floor, measuring the hem and putting pins in at the right length. Addy turned in a circle, taking tiny steps as the skirt of the dress was marked to the proper length. Then she took off the dress so Mrs. Ford could cut off the extra material.

When Mrs. Ford was finished, the long, wide piece of material she had cut from the bottom of the dress was hanging around her neck. Seeing it gave Addy an idea.

"Mrs. Ford, can I have the material you cut from the dress?" asked Addy.

"Certainly, Addy," replied Mrs. Ford. "All of this dress belongs to you. Now sit right down here and sew up the hem. You know how to do that. I'll be leaving now. But you can stay down here where the light is better and let your mother rest. When you're through, don't forget to put out the lamp."

"Yes, ma'am," said Addy. "And thank you, Mrs. Ford. Thank you for such a beautiful dress."

"You're welcome, Addy," said Mrs. Ford. "Merry Christmas."

On Christmas morning, the sun shone brightly.
Addy and Momma woke early, excited to spend their
first Christmas in freedom. Momma spoke first.
"I know you awake, bright eyes," she said. "Merry
Christmas."

"Merry Christmas, Momma," Addy said, sitting
up in bed. Sun streamed in the window, and the frosty
panes looked as though they were covered with a
delicate lace.

"I got a surprise for you, honey," said Momma.
She handed Addy a small parcel wrapped in paper.

"I got one for you, too, Momma," said Addy
excitedly.

"You open yours first," laughed Momma.

So Addy untied the string. As the paper fell away,
she saw a little rag doll with a bright red smile stitched
on her face. She had a bow tucked in her hair, tiny hoop
earrings, and a purple dress.

Addy beamed with joy. "Momma, she so pretty,"
she said happily, hugging the doll. "She just as pretty
as Janie was."

Momma smiled at Addy. "I stuffed her with some beans I saved."

Addy hugged the doll. The beans gave her a lumpy plumpness that Addy liked. "I'll call her Ida Bean," said Addy with a giggle. "Now, Momma, sit down and hide your eyes while I get my surprise for you. Don't look, because mine ain't wrapped." Addy hopped out of bed and went across the room to her school satchel. She took out the gift she'd hidden inside.

"Are your eyes still closed, Momma?" Addy asked before turning around.

"Sure enough," said Momma.

Addy ran across the floor and placed her gift on Momma's lap.

"Now you can open your eyes," said Addy.

When Momma looked down, there was a lovely scarf of beautiful green plaid before her. The edges were sewn with tiny perfect stitches and the ends were fringed.

"Addy! Where'd you get this?" asked Momma in surprise.

Addy told Momma all about the dress Mrs. Ford had repaired for her and about the extra material that was left when she cut off the bottom to make the dress fit Addy. "I spent yesterday afternoon hemming the dress and making the extra material into a scarf for you, Momma," Addy explained.

"Oh, Addy," said Momma gently, running her hands across the plaid. "It's beautiful. Ain't we gonna look fine going to church this evening?" Momma gave Addy a long hug. "I'm proud of my girl!" she said.

Ida Bean sat on Addy's lap while she and Momma had breakfast together. Then Addy put on her apron and propped Ida Bean in a chair so she could watch as Addy and Momma made sweet-potato pudding. There was some pudding left over, so Momma put it in a small pan.

"We can leave this one here and have it tomorrow," Momma said.

By the middle of the afternoon, the pudding was done, and its sweet spicy smell filled the tiny garret. Then Momma and Addy got ready for church. Addy wore her beautiful new dress, and Momma took time braiding and fixing Addy's hair. Momma put her new scarf around her neck and tied it in a big bow. Addy thought Momma had never looked more beautiful.

"I'm gonna take Ida Bean with me to show Sarah," said Addy, tucking her doll under her arm. Then Addy and Momma headed down the stairs and out to church.

As they got closer to church, the sun was setting. They could hear the organ music. When they opened the big doors to the church and stepped inside, Addy knew that Sarah had been right. The altar *did* look magical, with the manger scene and the silvery star shining high above.

Addy and Momma had just been seated when a loud chord blasted from the organ. The choir began to walk down the aisle singing "Joy to the World" in strong, happy voices. A glow filled the dark church as the choir marched in. Each member held a candle that cast shadows into the church. Addy watched for Sarah, who was at the front of the choir. Sarah turned and smiled at Addy. Addy gave a shy wave back. She felt tears run down her cheeks. She was crying because the church was so beautiful and the choir sounded so good and she and Momma were together.

When the service was over, everyone went down to Fellowship Hall for dinner. There was turkey and dressing, squash and greens, cornbread and applesauce.

Addy had never had so much food on her plate at one time. When it was time to go back for dessert, Addy ignored all the cakes and pies and headed straight for Momma's sweet-potato pudding in the shining black skillet. As she savored each smooth, sweet bite, she thought about Poppa, Sam, and Esther. *Maybe next Christmas,* she thought. *Maybe next Christmas we'll all be together, eating Momma's sweet-potato pudding.*

After dinner, the adults lingered over their coffee while the children hurried to the room set up for the shadow play. Sarah and Addy sat on a bench next to each other with Ida Bean snuggled between them. When all the children were settled, the door was closed. The lamps on the walls were blown out and the room was completely dark. The children squealed with excitement and pretended to be scared. After a minute, a lamp began to glow behind the sheet in front of the room. All eyes watched as the first shadow figure appeared on the sheet and the Christmas story was read aloud.

One figure and then another and another appeared on the sheet until soon Addy could see the shadow of Mary bent over the manger, holding her newborn baby, with Joseph standing at her side. Three shepherds stood beside them. A deep, rolling voice continued to read as all the children sat in the dark, quietly watching the shapes against the lighted sheet.

As the star appeared to guide the wise men, the door at the side of the room opened. A shaft of light from the hall filled the darkened room. The children turned to see who had opened the door. It was a tall man. Though Addy could not see his face, his shadow was a shape she recognized. Addy jumped up and struggled past the girl next to her, tripping over her feet, stumbling as she hurried to the door. Addy knew who was standing in the door, standing there right now, not in a dream, not someday, but right now.

"Poppa," she burst out. "Poppa, is that you?"

"Is that my Addy?" came the answer.

It was Poppa! Addy rushed to him and he swept her up into his strong arms and held her close for a long time.

It was dark by the time Addy, Poppa, and Momma headed back to the garret, walking hand in hand through the Christmas streets. When they got to the top of the stairs above Mrs. Ford's shop, Addy could see light under their door.

"That's strange," Momma said. "We didn't leave the candle burning."

When they opened the door, there on the table was a kerosene lamp shining brightly. Addy read the note lying beside it. "May the hope of the Christmas season shine in your lives always. Merry Christmas from Mrs. Ford," she read.

Poppa turned away from Addy.

"What's wrong, Poppa?" she asked. Then she heard him. He was crying.

"Don't cry," Addy said.

Poppa faced Addy and knelt down in front of her. "I'm crying because I'm so happy. I'm so proud you can read," he said. "I always knew you was a smart girl."

"Addy doing so good in school," Momma said. "She won a prize for spelling."

"Momma can read, too. And write," said Addy. "I been helping her, and I can help you."

"Come sit at the table, you two," Momma said. "I got something Poppa might like."

They sat down at the table and Momma brought the little pan of pudding that they'd set aside that morning.

"Sweet-potato pudding!" Poppa exclaimed. "Ruth, it was like you knew I was coming."

"We never stopped hoping," Momma said, smiling.

Addy picked up Ida Bean and crawled into Poppa's lap. Poppa ate the pudding while he told Addy and Momma about the time since he was taken from them.

"Me and Sam was separated that very next day. I don't know where they took him, but I think it was further south."

"Or maybe he escaped," Addy said hopefully.

"Maybe," Poppa said. "If there was a way for your brother to run, I know he found it. I couldn't though. I was bound hand and foot all the way to my new plantation. And after all that, all us slaves on the plantation was freed two months after I got there."

"And then you found your way to Momma and me," Addy said.

Then Momma and Addy told Poppa about leaving Esther with Auntie Lula and Uncle Solomon and escaping into the woods and on to freedom in Philadelphia. Poppa was quiet for a minute. Then he said, "I'm gonna try my best to get Esther and Sam back with us so we can all be together right here in Philadelphia like we planned. There was a freedmen's society in Maryland that helped me come here to you. Maybe the freedmen's society in Philadelphia can help us."

Addy laid her head against Poppa's chest. She felt certain that their dream would happen. "One day," she said, "we all gonna be together—all of us with Esther and Sam, too."

"You tired, Addy," Momma said. "It's time you got ready for bed."

"Can't I stay up longer?" Addy asked.

"You want to sit up all night like a little ol' owl?" Poppa teased.

Addy laughed. "Yes, Poppa. I want to stay up and be with you."

"Well, I ain't going nowhere. I'm gonna be here when you wake up in the morning," Poppa said. "I'll be the first thing you see when the sun comes in that window."

"Addy loved that window from the second we moved in here," Momma said, "but it got stuck about a month ago and we can't get it down."

"Let me have a look at it," Poppa said. He lifted Addy off his lap and went over to the window. Momma and Addy followed him. Poppa studied the window and then hit the frame in two places. Then he pulled down hard and closed the window.

"There!" said Poppa. "It needs a new sash. I can make that. But it should be warmer in here now."

"It already is," said Addy. She and Momma put their arms around Poppa. In the window, Addy could see their happy faces reflected in the glow of the lamplight.

INSIDE Addy's World

More than 300 years before Addy was born, the first black people arrived in America. Most came as slaves, brought on ships by slave traders. The traders had captured or bought them in Africa, taking them from their families, their tribes, and their homeland. In Africa they had a life rich in art, religion, music, and language. But in America they were forced to work against their will, without pay, for life.

By Addy's time, most enslaved people worked on *plantations*, or large farms, in the southern United States. Most slaves planted, tended, and harvested crops, but some were blacksmiths, shoemakers, and carpenters, or worked in their owners' houses as cooks, nursemaids, and seamstresses.

The treatment of slaves varied widely, but owners usually provided just enough food and clothing for slaves to survive. Most slaves lived in one-room cabins with dirt floors. Owners might punish them by whipping them, shackling their feet and hands, or making them eat tobacco worms, as Addy had to. Worst of all, owners could divide up and sell slave families, as Addy's owner did.

It was against the law in most southern states to teach African Americans to read and write. Even in the North where there was no slavery, black students were usually taught in separate schools from white students, as Addy was in Philadelphia. This separation is called *segregation*.

By the early 1800s, most northern states had made slavery illegal. And in 1808, it became illegal to bring slaves into the United States. But the buying and selling of slaves continued in the South until Addy's time.

People who were against slavery were called *abolitionists*. Abolitionists, both black and white, helped slaves escape on the Underground Railroad, a series of routes and hiding "stations" leading north to freedom. Escaping slaves traveled at night, hidden by darkness, usually to the northern states or Canada. Escaping required great courage, because runaway slaves who were caught were brutally punished.

When Addy and her mother escaped, northern states were fighting against southern states in the Civil War. This war had many causes, but one of the most important was the disagreement about slavery. People in the North felt slavery should not be legal. In 1861, several southern states *seceded,* or separated, from the United States. These states formed their own nation, called the Confederate States of America. President Abraham Lincoln believed it was wrong for the southern states to secede, and he eventually declared war against the South. That war was called the War Between the States, or the Civil War.

Lincoln's reason for declaring war was to keep the nation together, not to end slavery. But on January 1, 1863, Lincoln proclaimed that all slaves in states still fighting the North were *emancipated,* or free. Because the South had decided that it was a separate nation, it ignored the Emancipation Proclamation. That's why many people, like Addy's family, were still risking their lives to escape slavery in 1864.

Read more of ADDY'S stories,

available from booksellers and at *americangirl.com*

☺ *Classics* ☺

Addy's classic series, now in two volumes:

Volume 1:
Finding Freedom

In the midst of the Civil War, Addy and her mother risk everything to make a daring escape to freedom in the North.

Volume 2:
A Heart Full of Hope

As Addy's family makes a new life in Philadelphia, they find that freedom brings new chances—and has great costs.

☺ *Journey in Time* ☺

Travel back in time—and spend a day with Addy!

A New Beginning

Discover what Addy's life was like during the Civil War. Outrun a slave catcher, raise money for soldiers, and help Addy find her family. Choose your own path through this multiple-ending story.

☺ *Mysteries* ☺

More thrilling adventures with Addy

Shadows on Society Hill

Addy is overjoyed when Poppa's new boss invites Addy's family to live on his property in Philadelphia's elegant Society Hill neighborhood. But Addy soon discovers that their new home holds dangerous secrets—and one of them leads straight back to the North Carolina plantation she escaped only two years before.

A Sneak Peek at

A Heart Full of Hope

An Addy Classic

Volume 2

Addy's adventures continue in the
second volume of her classic stories.

The jump ropes slapped on the sidewalk as Addy took her place at the end of the line of girls who were playing Double Dutch after school. Addy had just missed for the fourth time.

"Don't worry," said her good friend Sarah. "Just keep trying. You'll get it. Double Dutch is hard."

Addy agreed. "It sure is. I can jump with one rope just fine. But the minute I try to jump into two, I get all tangled up. The ropes go so fast, I can hardly see them."

"That'll change," said Sarah. "Just don't get discouraged."

In spite of her troubles with Double Dutch, Addy felt happy on this pretty spring day. Poppa had been back with her and Momma for three months. They had moved out of Mrs. Ford's garret and into a boarding house. It was almost like having a big family again, except that Addy's brother Sam and baby sister Esther weren't there. *Maybe that'll change someday, too,* she thought.

"Look it there," Sarah said, pointing up the street. "Ain't that your poppa driving the ice wagon?"

Addy looked where Sarah was pointing. "That's

Poppa!" Addy exclaimed. "Let's go meet him." The girls took off and raced down the block.

"Well, well," Poppa said in his deep voice when the girls reached the wagon. "Look what the wind done blown my way. I reckon you girls could use a nice chunk of ice to cool you down."

"I sure could," said Sarah, panting from the run.

"Me, too," said Addy with a smile.

Poppa got down from his seat. The girls followed him to the back where he opened the doors of the wagon. Inside were huge blocks of ice. Addy could feel a moist coolness come from inside. Poppa slipped on a pair of thick gloves and took an ice pick from his belt. As he chipped away at a block of ice, glittering slivers flew into the air. He handed Sarah and Addy each a piece of ice the size of a small slice of pie.

"If you girls want a ride home, I'm gonna be heading that way in a bit. I got a few stops to make first," Poppa said.

"We'd like to ride. Come on, Sarah," Addy said.

"I can't," said Sarah. "I got to get right straight home and help my momma."

"All right," Addy said. "I'll see you tomorrow."

She was disappointed. Sarah often had to help her mother do the washing that she took in to earn money.

Addy and Poppa climbed onto the wagon as Sarah left. Poppa slapped the reins on the horse's back, and the wagon moved away from the curb.

Addy sat close to Poppa, sucking on her piece of ice. It was like holding a piece of winter. Addy had to shift it from hand to hand as it slowly melted and dripped. Poppa gave her his huge gloves.

"Wear these," he said, "so your hands won't get cold."

"I wish Sarah ain't have to help her momma so much," Addy said as she put the gloves on.

"I wish she didn't neither," Poppa said, "but her family need the money." He shook his head. "I never did expect things to be easy in freedom, but I didn't think things would be so hard either."

Addy looked at Poppa. His big smile had melted away. His face looked serious.

"When me and Momma first got here, I didn't like Philadelphia," Addy said softly. "Momma worked real hard, and I spent most of my time alone in our room. I was missing you and Sam and Esther something awful. But Momma kept saying things was gonna get better. It was gonna take time for things to change."

"Sometimes it seem like change is as slow as this here tired old horse," Poppa sighed. "But at least in Philadephia, things can change for the better."

"That's true," Addy said, finishing her ice and removing Poppa's gloves. "When we was down on the plantation, there was no chance for things to change."

"Slavery was draining the life out of all of us," said Poppa. "That's one reason I knew we had to take our freedom."

Addy spread out her arms. "Here in Philadelphia, it seem like my world getting bigger and bigger. Sometimes I can't believe I really go to school, that I can read and write and do my figures. I used to dream about it, but now it's real. And look at us, Poppa. We riding around the city on this big wagon! This is much better than worming tobacco plants."

Addy saw a smile ease back onto Poppa's face.

Poppa said, "There *is* some things better here. You going to school, me and your momma getting *paid* for our work, and we got a nice room at the boarding house."

"Even though Sam and Esther ain't with us yet," Addy said, "you being here done made things much better for me and Momma."

"But I want them to be even better," Poppa responded. "Hauling ice don't take nothing but muscle. I'm a good carpenter. I got a good mind. I can build anything. Every carpenter job I try to get, they say they don't hire colored folks. Ain't that something, Addy. When we was in slavery, I was a carpenter. Now that I'm free, I find out these white people up North think a colored man ain't good enough or smart enough to drive a nail."

"That ain't fair," Addy said.

"Sure ain't," Poppa said. "But that's the way it is."

Poppa made two deliveries before he came to his last stop at Natkin's Confectionery Shop. Addy could see a group of white girls about her age sitting at a table eating ice cream. She had walked by this shop once with Sarah, and Sarah had told her they sold ice cream there. Back then, Addy had not even known what ice cream was, but at a church social a few weeks later, Addy had her first taste of it. She loved it! It was creamy and sweet and cold. Without thinking, Addy blurted out to Poppa, "It sure would be good to have some ice cream now."

As soon as the words had flown out of her mouth, Addy felt awful. She shouldn't ask Poppa to spend money on fancy treats, and she also knew that this shop didn't serve black people. She looked again at the group of girls talking happily inside. Poppa glanced where Addy was looking. He didn't say anything as he climbed down from the wagon.

Addy watched Poppa lift a huge block of ice with a pair of large tongs. He rested it on his shoulder, headed down the alley, and went in the side door of the confectionery. On his way out, Poppa stopped to talk to a white man who gave Poppa a friendly pat on the shoulder.

"Was that Mr. Natkin?" asked Addy.

Poppa climbed back onto the wagon. "Yes," said Poppa. "I'm telling you, Addy, this is some kinda freedom. I can deliver ice to make ice cream, but I can't even buy my own daughter a dish of it."

"That's all right," Addy said. "I don't like it anyway."

Poppa looked at her out of the corner of his eye. Addy could tell he didn't believe her. "Let me make sure that door is closed," he said, jumping from the wagon.

When Poppa returned, he was carrying something. "Look here at what was in the trash," he said. "It's a busted-up ice cream freezer. I bet I can fix it up. Then we'll make our own ice cream." Poppa gave Addy a playful nudge. "Won't that be nice?" he asked.

"It would be," Addy said.

Poppa tugged on the reins, and the wagon gave a slow lurch forward.

Addy and Poppa rode on in silence. She was thinking, *Momma, Poppa, and I and all the colored people got a strange kind of freedom here in Philadelphia. There are jobs we can't get and shops we can't eat at just because of the color of our skin. It ain't fair.* When Addy thought of it, she felt just as dizzy as she had standing before the spinning loops of the Double Dutch ropes. Being a black girl in Philadelphia was like being outside the loops of those ropes. Inside was a world Addy wanted to enter. But right now, she was standing on the outside looking in. How would she be able to jump into that other world?

Meet the Author

CONNIE PORTER grew up near Buffalo, New York, where the winters are long and hard. As girls, she and her sisters trudged through deep snow to borrow books from the bookmobile that came to the neighborhood twice a week. After the girls finished their homework at night, they crawled into their beds and read the books aloud to each other. Ms. Porter still loves to read books. Today, she lives in Pennsylvania with her daughter.